"Those men with the guns," she said. "Do you think they'll follow us?"

Jake drew in a breath. If he'd dreamed there was ever a chance he could get her back, he was about to throw that all away with his next words.

"I wish I knew more about what to expect from them," he said. "But I do know this—there is no 'us.'"

That familiar wounded look swept across her, stabbing him in the heart. Again. He couldn't go through the pain with this woman one more time. "This is something I have to do alone. I'm taking you back as soon as it's safe."

Instead of a reply, Kelsey stared at the shattered window. Jake could feel the blood drain from his face as he considered that either one of them could have been hurt or killed just now.

"I don't know what you've gotten yourself into," she said, pressing her finger into a bullet hole in the canopy. "But it looks as if we're both in trouble here."

Books by Elizabeth Goddard

Love Inspired Suspense

Freezing Point
Treacherous Skies
Riptide

ELIZABETH GODDARD

is a seventh-generation Texan who grew up in a small oil town in East Texas, surrounded by Christian family and friends. Becoming a writer of Christian fiction was a natural outcome of her love of reading, fueled by a strong faith.

Elizabeth attended the University of North Texas, where she received her degree in computer science. She spent the next seven years working in high-level sales for a software company located in Dallas, traveling throughout the United States and Canada as part of the job. At twenty-five, she finally met the man of her dreams and married him a few short weeks later. When she had her first child, she moved back to East Texas with her husband and daughter and worked for a pharmaceutical company. But then, more children came along and it was time to focus on family. Elizabeth loves that she gets to do her favorite things every day—read, write novels, stay at home with her four precious children and work with her adoring husband in ministry.

RIPTIDE

ELIZABETH GODDARD

HARLEQUIN® LOVE INSPIRED® SUSPENSE

Recycling programs
for this product may
not exist in your area.

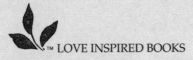

™ LOVE INSPIRED BOOKS

ISBN-13: 978-0-373-44547-9

RIPTIDE

Copyright © 2013 by Elizabeth Goddard

www.LoveInspiredBooks.com

Printed in U.S.A.

When you pass through the waters,
I will be with you; and when you pass through the
rivers, they will not sweep over you. When you
walk through the fire, you will not be burned;
the flames will not set you ablaze.
—*Isaiah* 43:2

To my Lord and Savior. You are my Shepherd.

Acknowledgments:

Every writer relies on expert resources to
fill in the blanks where their knowledge is weak.
Special thanks to Dr. Jan Hood for your encouragement
and support in reading through the scenes requiring
medical expertise and input. Thanks for bringing in
Dr. Randy Richter for his suggestions regarding my
war veteran medic, and thanks to Dr. Richard Mabry,
medical thriller author extraordinaire.

I needed their expertise to make sure things
could happen the way they did. In some cases,
I took artistic license for the sake of the story,
but where mistakes occur, they are my own.

ONE

What would it feel like to send high-voltage electrical currents through an intruder?

I hope I don't have to find out.

Kelsey Chambers wrapped her fingers around the electroshock device Captain Neely had left with her. Someone had boarded her boss's boat and started the engine. She'd spent enough time on *The Buccaneer* while working on her travel writing assignment to feel the subtle shift, recognize the rhythmic hum of the motor. It wouldn't be Captain Neely and his wife since they were on the island to celebrate their anniversary.

Sitting in the galley of the small but luxurious yacht, Kelsey left her laptop and the images she'd taken of the San Juan Islands and bounded up the steps.

Gripping the weapon, she stepped above deck into a dreary Pacific Northwest day. Angry voices shouted from the end of the secluded pier. Men ran toward *The Buccaneer*.

A bullet ricocheted too close for comfort.

"Get down!" a man yelled from behind.

Before she had a chance to face him, he shoved Kelsey to the ground at the same moment she fired the weapon, sending the charged projectiles into the air to connect with nothing. She cried out as her torso slammed against the deck, her knees taking the brunt of it. Where had he come from?

"Good thing you can't aim, lady, I'm trying to protect you!" Kelsey made to push up.

"Stay down," he hissed, and held her in place.

Another bullet flew by. Covering her head with her arms, she decided to take his advice. "What's going on?" she asked.

Ignoring her question, he held her down as if hoping the danger might pass if they waited long enough. Kelsey wasn't so sure. Peeking through the protection of her arms, she caught a glimpse of his Dodgers' baseball cap, sunglasses and then... Recognition squeezed her, crushing her breathless.

No... It couldn't be.

"Jake?" Confusion hit her like a squall. Jake Jacobson was the man she'd fallen hard for before they had ended their relationship a year ago. "What are you doing on *The Buccaneer?*"

From his awkward position next to her, Jake stared back in stunned silence, but then shouts from the pier grew louder and his expression turned dark.

"We have to hurry. Can you make it to the cockpit?"

"I'm not going anywhere with you!" Had she really just said that? This hardly seemed like the time to let their past stand in the way.

Hurt flickered across his gaze before it turned cold. "You will if you want to live."

Under the circumstances what choice did she have? Face the men shooting at them—might as well have been a firing squad—or leave with Jake. For a half second, she almost weighed the choices.

He nudged her toward the bow. On trembling knees she crawled forward, up the three steps and hunkered behind a captain's chair in the cockpit. All the while, more gunfire rang in her ears.

Who were these men, and why were they shooting at Jake? At her by default?

His back to her, he took the helm, steering *The Buccaneer* away from the dock. How had he managed the mooring single-handedly? He needed a code to activate the keyless ignition. Where did he get that? Too many questions bombarded her as everything happened within a fifteen-second span of time. Her mind finally wrapped around the fact that Jake was leaving the dock and taking her with him.

She was being swept right along with the boat.

Lord, how do I get out of this?

Still, to flee the boat while several men shot at them wasn't an option. They had to get away from the gunfire, and she wouldn't stand in Jake's way as he ferried them to safety.

Or was she making a huge assumption here thinking the men at the pier were the threat to her safety rather than Jake?

Escape now. Ask questions later.

A window in the cockpit shattered. A scream tore from Kelsey's throat, as if her voice had a life of its own, and she hunkered even lower, wrapping her arms tightly around her head.

The Buccaneer accelerated, transporting Jake and Kelsey away from the dock and the marina.

"We're out of range now," Jake said. "You can get up."

Slowly unfolding from her position, she stood to face him. "What…what are you doing here? What's this all about?" she demanded. The more she thought about it, though, it seemed apparent Jake was on the run and had stolen *The Buccaneer* as his means of escape, Kelsey his accidental passenger.

Or was she? He'd seemed surprised to see her on deck, but he could have been faking. Was abducting her part of his plan all along?

He pulled his sunglasses off and glanced her way. Wow. She'd forgotten how he could overwhelm her with those blue eyes. Right now they were the same brooding color of a stormy Pacific Ocean. But he looked different somehow.

"Kelsey?" Jake squeezed his eyes shut and opened them like he'd gotten something in them. "I thought I was seeing things before."

Right. Always the kidder.

That's all he could say after a year? He could put on a good act, or he no longer cared about her. Either way, he had some explaining to do.

Another boater laid on his horn in warning, and Jake returned his attention to maneuvering *The Buccaneer* completely out to sea.

Kelsey eyed the marina growing distant behind them, confused about what had just happened. "I asked you a question. What are you doing?"

"I'm taking this boat, what does it look like?"

"But why? You want to tell me why someone was shooting at you? At us? Why you're stealing this boat?" His explanation had better be good.

Jake cut her a quick glance then focused on the open waters of the Salish Sea between Washington and Canada. Storm clouds brewed in the distance and the wind picked up, the boat shifting as the water swelled with whitecapped waves.

She'd spent the last good-weathered weekend in the San Juan Islands, finishing out this assignment, and up until ten minutes ago, it looked like she had timed things just right. But how could she have planned for this? She arched a brow, waiting for Jake's response.

"Yeah, about that. I'm sorry," he offered. "I'm not stealing the boat. Just returning it to its rightful owner. I'd planned to make sure no one else was on board when out of nowhere those men started shooting, and then you showed up. I didn't wait around to ask them why, and I couldn't exactly shove you off board into a gunfight, could I? So you're along for the ride. At least for the moment."

He tossed her a half grin, but she could tell he wasn't any happier with the situation than she was.

More likely, though, *his* reaction had everything to do with being shot at and nothing at all to do with her. A guy like him? He must have moved on already.

An old, familiar ache traced across her heart. She shook off the unwanted melancholy and focused her attention back on the present.

Jake must be in some kind of trouble. That scared her, but she'd picked up the pieces of her heart long ago and couldn't afford to get involved now. Could she? No. Definitely not. In fact, if he was getting shot at, that meant she'd made the right decision when she'd ended their relationship.

"What's going on here, Jake? Really. And I want a straight answer."

He drew in a breath. "Three months ago I boarded this same cruiser yacht in order to reclaim it for the bank. It carries a hefty price tag so it's worth my time."

"Doesn't the boat belong to *Hidden Passage Travel Magazine?*"

"No. It used to belong to the magazine's owner, Davis Burroughs, but he defaulted on his loan."

Kelsey found it hard to believe that her new boss's boat was being repossessed. Was Davis in some sort of financial trouble? The magazine was thriving, wasn't it? And the last she knew of Jake, he still worked as a commercial pilot for Journey Airlines. Now he was some kind of repo man? None of this made any sense. "So, why didn't you take it *then?*"

"I tried to play nice, that's why, and explained why I was taking the boat. I faced off with an older couple and a few of their friends and ended up thrown into the warm water off the coast of Baja. Now that I finally located her again, I wasn't about to risk getting tossed this time and planned to take her when she was empty." Jake shut off the engine and allowed the boat to drift. "That part of my plan didn't work so well, considering you were on board."

"You might have looked first, ya know?"

"I already told you, I didn't get the chance." After scrambling around in a few compartments, he found binoculars, then peered through them, searching the water, the swells growing with the approaching storm.

Kelsey hoped they were heading back to land soon.

A hint of nausea swam in her stomach. She hadn't faced much of that on this assignment because she'd only traveled within the Inside Passage—the waterway that weaved in and out of islands, protecting travelers from the harsh waters of the open Pacific all the way to Alaska.

"Are you looking for those men who were shooting? You still haven't explained about that." Kelsey wasn't sure she wanted to know the answer, but she had to ask.

"I can't explain what I don't know. I've never seen those men before today. I can only guess that Burroughs must have hired them to keep anyone from trying to repossess the boat."

He lowered the binoculars and looked at her. Really looked at her this time. He acted like he was drinking her in after he hadn't seen her in months. That was the reaction she'd expected and maybe even wanted, but then again, maybe his first reaction was better, considering they were no longer a couple. His gaze drifted over her face, lingered on her lips a few seconds too long and then locked with her eyes.

Her pulse went haywire.

No. Definitely Not. You are not getting involved with him again. Forget that there hadn't been a day since they'd parted ways that she hadn't thought about him. And why, now that she thought she'd found a way to move on, he had suddenly showed up.

A familiar tangle of hot emotion twisted in her throat.

She needed to get off this boat and away from him and whatever he was involved in. And what if Jake wasn't telling her the truth? What if he really was *stealing* the boat? Would Davis hold her responsible for letting Jake take it?

The electroshock weapon Captain Neely had left with her made more sense in this context.

"Now you can answer a few of *my* questions," he said.

"What are you doing here anyway? Did you know you're with someone who has gone to a lot of trouble to hide this yacht for months now? Someone who's apparently willing to kill to keep her from being taken away? Being with someone like that puts you in danger." Jake crossed his arms and peered at her from under his cap. "Tell me what you know."

Her in danger? Davis authorizing the use of deadly force? Something wasn't adding up. Jake was trying to turn things around on her. He had some nerve.

Kelsey took a few lengthy breaths, battling her erratic heartbeat. "I don't know anything. It has to be some sort of mistake."

On your part, no doubt.

She left Jake's side to look for the shock device she'd dropped. Davis had sent her on this trip, knowing that someone wanted to reclaim the yacht. That was a big disappointment in itself. Kelsey sighed. Travel writing was supposed to help her fulfill her dream of seeing the world, and she had hoped it would help her forget about Jake, too.

If only she hadn't ignored the niggling thoughts that told her this job was too good to be true. More than anything, she'd wanted it to be true. After all, chances like this only came along once in a lifetime. Yeah. That's exactly what she'd thought when she'd fallen in love with the man of her dreams—the man right in front of her.

And the job of her dreams had led her right back into his path. Not only that, but apparently the moment she'd climbed aboard *The Buccaneer,* she'd stepped into danger.

Jake's mind reeled at seeing Kelsey again. His heart, too. But he couldn't let her know that. So he tried to act indifferent while he figured things out.

Even though he'd seen the two-person crew leaving the boat earlier in the day, Jake knew to check all the compartments before departing the marina. After flying off with an unwanted passenger the first time he'd participated in a repo, he'd had all the experience he ever wanted with that. But here he was again. And had Jake put her in danger today? Or was she already in danger and he'd come along at just the right time, saving her from harm?

All questions remaining to be answered.

The Buccaneer was beginning to look like more trouble than she was worth. The high-end repossession gig was an adrenaline rush, but the edge of danger in this case had gone too far. And for once, the job was doing nothing to help him with his other goal—keeping his mind off things he wanted to forget. Make that people he wanted to forget.

Or better…the one person he had wanted to forget, and the fact she had broken his heart. That's what he got for letting himself fall for her. Love and commitment. It was all over-rated. The pain that came with a breakup canceled out anything positive. And even when you tried to forget someone, they managed to turn up in your life again and wash away the progress you had made on trying to forget.

He certainly hadn't planned on seeing Kelsey Chambers again, especially on board *The Buccaneer*. He had thought he'd left her behind for good. Seeing her now reminded him of all his failures, and yet—looking at her stirred up memories of so much more.

She stood before him now, graceful as the day he'd first seen her on that beach in Hawaii. Ash-blond hair perfectly framed her pretty face. Her striking hazel eyes with their exotic slant pinned him in place. She was the only woman he'd ever fallen for. Yet this time, she wore a guarded expression.

Jake took a weighty step back. A knot grew in his throat. Why did his pulse have to race at the sight of her?

"Who are you to Burroughs anyway?" he asked. "His girlfriend?"

Brilliant. His tone was anything but friendly and that made it sound like he still cared.

"What?" Her arms stiffened at her sides. "Davis is my boss, as if it's any of your business."

"You're right. I'm surprised to see you, that's all. I thought you worked for an airline magazine."

"I took a travel writing job a few weeks ago. I was just about to finish off an assignment exploring the Inside Passage. It was supposed to end in Puget Sound. Obviously, your appearance changes that."

The way she dragged out that last line, and the accompanying negative tone, begged for an apology from him, and without thinking, he gave one. "I'm sorry."

And those two little words echoed what he'd told her the day she'd broken things off with him. How many ways would she make him apologize this time? His gut felt like a storm anchor had lodged there. He wasn't sure he could be in the same room with her without going through the pain all over again.

Creases appeared in her forehead, making her look a little older than her twenty-eight years. But she'd be twenty-nine by now. Was he supposed to remember her birthday when they weren't together? Whether he was supposed to or not, he remembered all right—that had been the day he'd decided to start training for an Ironman Triathlon, to put himself through grueling workouts if that's what it took to forget.

She watched him, appearing to contemplate his apology. Probably thinking about the last time she'd heard those words from him, same as he was.

"Those men with the guns," she said. "Do you think they'll follow us?"

Jake drew in a breath. His next words should be chosen carefully. They could have a significant effect on the outcome of…what, he wasn't sure. But if he ever dreamed in a moment of weakness that there was a chance he could get her back, he was about to throw that all away with his next words.

"I wish I knew more about what to expect from them," he said. "But I do know this—there is no 'us.'"

The double meaning in his words slammed him. That familiar wounded look swept across her features and ricocheted back, stabbing him in the heart. Again. He couldn't go through the pain with this woman one more time. "This is something I have to do alone. I'm taking you back as soon as it's safe. Or I can drop you off at the marina of your choice."

Instead of a reply, Kelsey stared at the shattered window. Her gaze traveled around the cockpit, looking for what? Bullet holes? Jake could feel the blood drain from his face as he considered that either one of them could have been hurt or killed just minutes ago.

Seeing her for the first time in months had shocked him, but seeing that she was in danger sent his pulse rocketing. He didn't know if he could take being the one to blame for her getting hurt.

"I don't know what you've gotten yourself into," she said, pressing her finger into a bullet hole in the canopy. "But it looks like we're both in trouble here. We both need to leave this boat."

Had he detected a hint of concern? Now that was something new. Ugh. Why did seeing her now have to affect his whole attitude?

"This is the fun part of my new job. My brother Connor and I own our own company now, recovering stuff with high price tags that are in arrears like your boss's yacht here—worth 1.7 million dollars. We get paid well for what we do. Therefore, I'm not going anywhere without this boat. Here's the fun part for you—you get to go back to the marina."

"You don't fly anymore, or work for Journey Airlines?"

Hadn't she heard anything he just said? "Oh, I fly, but not for Journey."

Somewhere in the distance, the high-pitched whine of accelerating motors announced approaching boats. He peered through the binoculars again. Two speedboats raced straight toward them. Had to be the men from the marina. But why?

"Time's up. We've got to go."

Jake started *The Buccaneer* again and headed back to shore. He should never have stopped, but he'd wanted to focus on Kelsey for a few minutes. He couldn't believe someone would chase him down like this.

Unless there was something more going on here than a dispute about a defaulted loan.

"Where are we headed now?" Kelsey had taken the binoculars and watched the boats drawing closer.

"I already explained. You're going back to the marina."

"That's fine by me. I didn't want to come along to begin with, remember?"

"I remember, all right." After all, why would she want to go anywhere with Jake, a man she'd claimed to love all those months ago?

The yacht bounced across the increasingly rough waters of the Salish Sea, making for a bumpy ride, even on a vessel this size. Considering that men were pursuing Jake, the yacht, or Kelsey—and he wasn't sure which yet—returning to the same marina where other men could be waiting might not be the safest place. And he didn't have a clue how to drop her off and make sure she was safe while keeping the boat like he'd so boldly proclaimed. He was making this up as he went.

Jake headed for a different marina down a few miles at Fisherman's Bay. He cut a few intermittent glances at Kelsey. Her dark blond hair whipped in the wind, though they were fairly protected behind the glass at the helm. At least that window hadn't been shot out.

"You sure you don't know anything about Burroughs or why he'd fight so hard to keep the boat?"

"Maybe they think you're kidnapping me," she said.

He caught a glimpse of her wry grin. "Ah, so you *are* a member of a wealthy family who's willing to pay a big ransom, and you were just holding out on me before."

If only wealth had been the problem to come between

them—that was something easily overcome. He considered a second teasing comeback, *and how do you know I'm not kidnapping you?* but caught another glimpse that told him she wasn't happy with his first reply. He was more than relieved he hadn't added fuel to that fire.

Just stick to the facts, and drop the flirting, will you? Problem was, it came all too naturally, and in the end had cost him everything. Hard to believe what he once thought was his *everything* was standing right next to him now. Second chances were hard to come by. Could this be one for them? Again, he clamped down on the stray thoughts attempting to emerge from the deep oceans of his heart. He'd long ago sunk his feelings for her and made sure they were weighted down, never to surface again. What was going on?

Clearing his throat, he yanked his focus back to the moment.

"In my experience," he said, "this isn't the normal course of business for law-abiding citizens who've fallen behind in their finances."

"What's considered normal, then?"

"Loans for things like cars, boats and even airplanes, allow the banks to take back their collateral, which gives me the right to go wherever I need to go, as a repo man, without being considered a trespasser. The way it works best is to move covertly before anyone's the wiser because sometimes it can be dangerous, especially when the property is worth millions. But I never expected to see guns on this one, I promise you."

Neither did he expect to see Kelsey.

"They're gaining on us," she said.

"No kidding. This thing maxes out at forty knots. We can't outrun them."

"What are we going to do? Can't you call the coast guard? The sheriff?"

"Sure, but even if I make the call, I think we're on our own. They can't make it in time." Jake reached for the VHS radio and turned to channel sixteen. "Mayday, Mayday, Mayday, this is—"

Gunfire dinged across the cockpit and Jake ducked, but the radio was toast.

Man, that was close. He glanced at Kelsey, glad she'd laid low.

"So what do we do now?"

"As soon as we hit the marina, I'll do my best to get near the dock, but I'm not going to take time with the mooring. Once we're close enough, we're going to jump for it. In other words we're going to abandon ship."

"Are you crazy?"

"A little bit."

And not because they were going to jump, but because he was actually going to leave the boat that he'd worked for months to locate. If Kelsey weren't in the picture, he might just consider risking it, but with these men chasing them, adding a woman into the mix was a recipe for disaster. Bottom line was: he still couldn't be certain the boat was what they were after. He couldn't leave her to face the possible danger alone. Things were definitely not adding up here.

As much as he hated to give the boat up, he couldn't stay on *The Buccaneer*. He would have to let her go for the second time.

Gunfire pinged against the back of the boat, sending adrenaline coursing through his veins. He had to get Kelsey out of this.

TWO

Kelsey ducked. "Can't you go any faster? They're gaining on us!"

"Stay low," Jake said, keeping his voice calm for Kelsey's sake. "The marina is up ahead."

"Up ahead is not close enough. The boats are closing in—one on each side of us."

"I'll try to outmaneuver them long enough to keep them from boarding us. Just keep low in case they start shooting again, okay?"

"Okay."

The whir of the motorboats overwhelmed Kelsey as Jake steered left in a wide swath, spraying the boat on the starboard side, and then right again. The force practically threw her against the wall, and then an abrupt, jarring impact told her he'd bumped one of the speeders on the port side.

Hunkered down, she clung to the chair, ducking behind it much as she'd done before when the men had shot at them. As Jake continued with the zigzag maneuvers, the familiar swirl of motion sickness rolled in her stomach. The speedboats with men chasing and shooting at them didn't help.

But at least Jake had thrown the men off for the moment and they were too busy steering their boats to shoot. She could call the police. They had to have a marine patrol. Something. Kelsey attempted to get at her cell, but in her current squatting position, she couldn't get it from her pants pocket without standing. She couldn't stand on this ride.

She crawled into the captain's chair and straightened enough to slide her hand into her pocket.

Jake glanced back at her. "I don't want you to get shot. Why don't you just go below deck?"

"No way. I couldn't stand it down there—the motion sickness would kill me before a bullet."

At her words, a slug whizzed by. Jake dropped and Kelsey bolted from the seat. She'd gotten her cell. The yacht made a wide arc, knocking Kelsey against the wall again, and her cell from her hand. It slid across the deck along with the shock device.

"What are you doing?" She yelled the question, not bothering to hide her frustration.

"Saving us, that's what." The Dodgers' cap set aside, he'd shoved his sunglasses on top of his head and stared straight ahead, slowing *The Buccaneer*. "Get ready. I don't think these jerks are going to tail me too closely into the marina. They don't want to draw more attention than they already have. And that's the only thing going for us right now."

"What do you mean? They shot at us, for crying out loud. I don't think they care about drawing attention." Granted, the other marina was pretty secluded. She couldn't say for sure if anyone was even around to hear the gunfire or take note of what happened.

"Just work with me here, will you? We're going to make a run for it."

"And then what?"

"We'll head straight for the San Juan County Sheriff's Office. There's a substation located near the marina. That's one of the reasons I thought we should head this way."

Considering all the mayhem and now she hadn't seen anything resembling law enforcement coming to their aid, his reassurances fell short of comforting Kelsey. Jake slowed the

yacht to the required speed and steered into the marina filled
with boats. Kelsey made to stand.

"Stay down." Jake shot her a warning glare. "They're right
behind us."

"Are you sure we shouldn't have taken our chances elsewhere?"

"Just where do you suggest?"

Good point. "But this just seems so crazy."

"This is going to be close," he said. "Another boat's passing me, headed out of the marina, so the men have backed
off, but not for long."

The yacht drifted slowly, rocking up and down with water
increasingly agitated by the approaching storm and passing
boats. Kelsey's palms grew moist. The next few moments
could mean life or death. And the crazy part was that she
didn't even know why. There had to be much more going on
here than Jake was telling her.

She hated to think of him lying to her—but that was the
whole reason she'd broken things off with him to begin with.
Kelsey had issues with trust thanks to a philandering father,
and she was always suspicious of Jake. Always fearing that
he was lying about where he'd been. What he was doing.
And it drove them both crazy until the grand finale of their
relationship.

Now here she was again in an unimaginable situation,
wondering if Jake was lying to her.

"I need to go below and grab my things."

"Now who's the crazy one? There's no time for that."

"My laptop. My camera. All my work. Everything. I can't
leave them behind."

"They're not worth your life, Kelsey. Just for the record,
I didn't want to do this, but I'm leaving this boat behind to
get us out safely. So you're not risking both of our lives for
your stuff. Got it?"

Her throat went dry. *He's leaving this boat behind for me?*

He shouldn't do her any favors, and she almost replied, giving him a few bitter words, though he didn't deserve them. Not now. She felt the gentle bump when *The Buccaneer* brushed against the pier and rocked gently. She found her cell on the deck, though not the weapon Captain Neely had left behind. A big boat like this and Jake had brought it in for a smooth "landing" even under pressure.

She was impressed. But then she'd already experienced his expertise when it came to maneuvering boats, planes and women alike. She cringed inside. That hadn't been fair. She hated the resentment boiling under the surface.

Jake threw a nylon rope from the boat around a post. "I know what I said about leaving the mooring to someone else," he said, then winked, "but I don't want anyone to get hurt if the boat drifts."

How could the guy be playful at a time like this? But his charm never failed to send her heart dancing, even when it shouldn't, considering their past.

"Ready?" He held out his hand. "Don't worry. You'll get your stuff back. Let's go."

She took his hand, allowing him to pull her to her feet. His grip was strong and sturdy, just like she remembered, but it magnified just how feeble her heart remained where he was concerned. They left the helm and hopped from the boat onto the dock. Her heart still waltzed when he grabbed her hand again and together they ran the length of the dock.

Kelsey was almost afraid to look behind her as if seeing that the men were still after them would somehow seal their fate.

Jake squeezed Kelsey's hand and pulled her with him behind a fishing boat. Then he peeked around it to see if the men were following, or if they'd taken *The Buccaneer*. They'd sure seemed to want it badly enough.

He hated giving the yacht up, but he shouldn't have to risk his life or someone else's.

Especially the woman he…what? Loved? *Get over it.*

Apparently, he hadn't done a very good job of getting over Kelsey already.

"See anything?" Kelsey asked, her warm breath fanning his ear.

He turned and her beautiful face was close, not even an inch from his. Her eyes grew wide. She eased back to what she considered a safe distance. He suppressed a laugh. If he wanted to kiss her, she wasn't nearly far enough away.

A kiss might be nice about now, and that brought on a grin, but it also brought on a mental kick in the rear. *What are you thinking?* Would it always be like this? Him losing his mind when she was near?

"I don't see them anywhere," he said. "They moored their boats out of sight. Maybe they're already onboard *The Buccaneer* and below deck."

She sighed. "What do they want?"

Jake studied her, hating the thought niggling him, but it had been bugging him for a while now and he couldn't keep it to himself any longer. "They *are* after Burroughs's yacht, aren't they?" he asked. "You're sure they aren't after you?"

Kelsey's lips parted, but she hesitated, then finally said, "Very funny. I was thinking the same thing about you. Everything was great until you showed up."

Jake frowned. She was right of course.

He wasn't sure what to make of it. "Let's get out of here. Get to the substation. We can tell them everything and let them figure it out."

After a quick glance behind him, Jake started toward Fisherman's Bay Road where the substation was located. He made it his business to know about the law enforcement where he would be retrieving property and was especially grateful for his diligence this time. Fishermen and boat owners bustled about, securing their rigs for the approaching storm. A busy marina would go a long way in helping them elude the men, if they were even still after them.

When he and Kelsey made the road, they kept to the side and away from the occasional passing vehicles.

Kelsey tugged the cell from her pocket. "I should give Davis a call to let him know what's happened to his boat. And Captain Neely. He's on the island somewhere with his wife."

Jake stopped.

"What is it?" Kelsey asked, pausing next to him. She didn't wait to hear his answer but started searching her cell for contact numbers.

"Don't." Jake pressed his fingers against her wrist.

She dropped her hand to her side. "Why not?"

"Think about it. Those men want the boat or something on it. That means that either Burroughs or Neely has to know about whatever they want. Maybe both of them. You can't trust them."

He was pushing it with her, he knew, because she probably didn't think she could trust him, either.

"You want the boat, too," she said, a challenge in her tone. "Maybe you want the same thing. You're after it, too."

Ah, there it is. He lifted his hands in surrender. More like exasperation.

"Please tell me you get why I want the boat. There is only one bank that owns it, and I'm the only guy hired to collect it. Not those men who chased us down. Get it?"

Or do you think I'm lying? He couldn't bring himself to voice the question; invite more antagonism into the chaos. They needed to work together now. He needed to gain her trust this time, for this situation, somehow, and on that point, he didn't think he would win this race.

He'd do well to remember his training mantra.

Head, guts, heart.

Run the first ten miles with your head, the second with

your guts and the final miles with your heart. If he did this right, he'd keep his heart out of it.

"So you say." Kelsey pinned him with those exotic hazel eyes.

He hated the way they seemed to see right through him. Accusing. Cutting. And yet he loved the way they wrapped around his soul.

Caressing. Intoxicating.

He shook off the way she affected him—it didn't make up for the pain her words had caused.

"Okay, I'll just be honest with you here. That hurt."

To his surprise, a small grin rose in her left cheek. "I'm with you in wondering what's really going on."

"So you believe me?"

She twisted her lips into a half smile. "I shouldn't have toyed with you like that. I...I believe you."

Jake knew what that had cost her, but he hadn't expected how much it would mean to him. Tightness swelled in his chest. He couldn't respond, the words caught in his throat. Besides, he didn't want to ruin the moment. On the other hand, why couldn't she have believed him when it really mattered? At least for them as a couple.

"I don't know, though," she said and glanced off in the distance. "I can't believe Davis or Captain Neely are involved in something with those men. Men who are willing to kill. Maybe there's another reason."

"The reason doesn't matter. You're already in harm's way as it is. Don't call either of them. Let's wait and see what the sheriff's office has to say. In fact, let's get them to send someone with us back to the boat to get your things. We can take the ferry to Washington together and just leave the boat until this is all settled." Was he being presumptuous and overbearing? He watched her reaction.

"If Davis knew something like this might happen and he

sent me on the writing assignment…" She shook her head like she couldn't wrap her thoughts around it.

With the wind picking up, Jake wished he could wrap his arms around *her*. She didn't have on a jacket and neither did he. While the day had been warm and friendly earlier, Jake almost felt like he'd ushered in the inclement weather.

He sighed. They could buy jackets in town.

"You said you started your job a few weeks ago. How well do you know this guy?" he asked.

"We hung out at a museum together a lot. We became quick friends because we're both editors at magazines. He needed a travel writer, and I wanted something new in my life."

Something new in her life?

Her gaze slowly crept up to lock with his. Was she thinking about her slip, an unintentional reference to her need to move on since their big breakup? He sure was. Still, he would have thought she'd finished moving on from him long ago.

A ruckus along the pier startled his thoughts back to their current predicament where they needed to stay.

Jake pressed his hand at the small of her back, urging her forward. "We should walk while we sort this out." They needed to get to the substation. "Just to be clear, I don't plan to leave your side until this is over."

She was the one to stop this time and looked at him. "Until this is over?"

The question hung between them.

Once again, his words seemed to hold deeper meaning. When this was over, he'd never see her again. That was for the best. No doubt there. The only reason she was with him now was because of their chance meeting—what he did for a living had collided with what she did for a living.

But they'd both almost been gunned down for reasons unknown.

And those kinds of reasons were the worst kind.

THREE

Thunder crackled in the distance. Jake looked at the darkening sky just in time for a cloudburst to dump rain in his face. Spotting a burgundy canvas awning nearby, he ran for shelter with Kelsey.

Marble-sized raindrops pounded them, leaving them drenched as they ran, mud splattering their legs and shoes. He didn't think he could be wetter had he jumped into the Salish Sea. And this was only the beginning of the rainy season.

His back against the wall of a bike shop, he caught his breath and watched Kelsey shiver. He tried the door of the business but it was locked. A notice informed patrons the shop would reopen in twenty minutes. A couple empty blocks separated the store from the next building that might offer them shelter from the downpour.

"I wish I could give you my jacket," he said. "But I'm not wearing one."

She sent him a weak grin.

"Come here." Jake offered the warmth of his arms, knowing how dangerous that might be to his heart. But he could hardly stand by and watch her suffer.

Brows knitted, she gave a shake of her head. "No, that's all right. I'm a big girl."

Suit yourself. Jake felt like an idiot now. She'd certainly put him in his place.

The rain continued to pound the pavement and grass, crushing autumn flowers and weeds into the ground. One thing he knew about this region of the Pacific Northwest was that once the rainy season started, it wouldn't let up for months.

"Should we make a run for it?" he asked. "The substation is just a few blocks away."

"Let's wait. This should ease up a little." Kelsey rubbed her arms. "But is your offer still good?"

Now it was Jake's opportunity to put her in her place, but he didn't have the heart to turn her down. Despite her claim that she was a big girl, she sounded like a small child in need of nurturing. Plus, her lips were turning blue.

"Always." *Always?* Good one. He lifted his arm, inviting her in.

Kelsey leaned into him, and he wrapped her in his embrace, rubbing her chilled arms. After a while, the shivering stopped and she relaxed.

"Better?" he asked.

Her cheek against his chest, she nodded. He had to admit, he felt much warmer, too. But now he was suffering in another way instead. All the feelings he had for her came rushing back, though they'd never gone too far. Funny how he and Kelsey so readily fell back into this position—how natural it was. Like they hadn't just spent months apart trying—and in his case, failing—to forget each other.

"You've been working out," she murmured against his chest.

He chuckled. She probably wouldn't guess the reason he'd plunged himself into training for a triathlon.

"What happened to us, Kelsey?" As soon as the question left his mouth, he realized it was a mistake. Especially since he was well aware of the answer. He frowned. What was he doing, letting her in like this? He'd known better than to let down his guard.

She stiffened against him.

Jake feared he'd ruined everything. That she would step from his arms.

And that's exactly what she did. Kelsey stared at him.

"Really, Jake? You want to hash through that again *now?* What is it with you?" She huffed. "Men are all alike."

Kelsey stomped away from him and out into the deluge, leaving him under the awning alone. He really was an idiot. He followed her.

A puppy dog of an idiot.

"I know," he shouted out in the rain. "It's all about your father who cheated on your mother. So you can't trust anyone, especially not me. But, Kelsey, I can't change who I was before I met you. You don't seem to get that I never cheated on anyone, especially not you. I know how it looked that night, but if you could just find it in yourself to believe me on this…"
That would change everything.

Everything.

Why, oh, why, was he going up this river again? The current was too strong. What happened to attaching an anchor to his feelings for her and sending them to the Mariana Trench— the deepest part of the ocean, as far as his heart was concerned. Looked like those feelings had breached the water's surface now. This tempest of a situation had stirred up the ocean floor, the dark places in his soul.

He wanted to ask her for another chance, but clamped down on his brief moment of insanity. He knew exactly where that would take him and he wasn't willing to go there again. Ever. And he'd keep reminding himself of that finality no matter how many times it took.

She marched ahead of him. If he didn't think her life could be in danger, and maybe even his own, he would just let her march until she was out of sight. Just like he had last year.

From the start, Kelsey had struggled with his past. So he'd dated a lot of women. Maybe he'd earned a less-than-stellar reputation as not exactly husband material. Maybe he was just looking for the right one in all the wrong places. But he should have known that when the right one finally came along, she'd be the kind of girl who wanted to be the only one.

Why couldn't the woman understand that she *was* the only one? The only one for Jake, at least. He couldn't help it if almost everywhere they went he ran into someone he'd dated.

Kelsey couldn't take it, and considering her father, Jake couldn't exactly blame her. They'd almost worked through their problems when everything fell apart that one night. The mental images sent spasms through his gut.

The pain and the memories overturned his momentary emotional slip. He felt it all over again like it was happening fresh—especially watching Kelsey moving away from him now.

He couldn't change his past, but he could control his future. He had every intention of having a future without more heartbreak.

Splashing through the puddles and torrent, Jake ground his molars and shoved aside his issues of the heart to focus on the present. After he delivered Kelsey to the sheriff and told his story, he wasn't so sure their ferry ride together back to Seattle was going to happen.

Kelsey had no intention of engaging in this particular conversation with Jake.

Fury burned like acid in her throat. At least, it warmed her cheeks and kept the cold rain from making her shiver again. She couldn't believe he'd asked her what had happened. Why did she have to go through this all over again?

She couldn't just forget her father's philandering and Jake's past. Asking her to believe him about Heather, a glamorous, gorgeous woman who Kelsey had seen leaving his apartment, was asking too much. She wanted to believe him. But she'd watched her mother ignore her father's cheating for years.

Kelsey would not look the other way and yet, her resolve had created a jealous and suspicious monster. Even when she had managed to shove aside her suspicions, the whole situation just magnified everything wrong in her relationship with him.

No. Kelsey needed a man who didn't attract the opposite sex like a supercharged magnet. A man who hadn't played the field like a trophy-winning World Cup soccer player.

The sheriff's office came into view, steering her focus back where it should be.

"I see the substation just across the street," she said loud enough for Jake to hear behind her and jogged ahead of him, not caring if he followed.

Kelsey was trying to start a new life, live her dreams, forget about her failures. Then all *this* had to happen. She had the feeling that Jake wasn't behind her, after all. And she did care. They were in this together. Wasn't the plan to head to the sheriff's substation? In the middle of the street Kelsey whirled around, confirming Jake was gone.

The torrent let up, easing into a drizzle.

"Jake?"

You've got to be kidding me! He left? Just like that? He was a real class act.

Jake stepped from the corner of a building across the street, a knife held at his throat by someone behind him in the building's shadow. He gave a subtle shake of his head.

His eyes told her to run.

Just as suddenly as he'd appeared, he disappeared behind the wall. Kelsey's heart hammered against her ribs. Those men had some nerve, taking Jake in front of the sheriff's office. The substation was *right* behind her.

Twenty-five yards, maybe. She could get help and quickly. But they would be the twenty-five longest yards she'd ever traveled, considering the knife pressed against his throat.

Lord, what do I do now?

Jake had told her that her laptop and camera, things she'd left on the boat, weren't worth her life. Maybe not, but Jake was worth everything she could do to save him. If she left him behind now and found safety and shelter inside the San Juan County Sheriff's Office, Jake would die and Kelsey would never forgive herself.

That much was clear. Leaving him was out of the question.

A horn blared and the chrome grill of a bus loomed in her vision. Kelsey took off jogging toward where she'd seen Jake. Before she made the corner, someone grabbed her, covering her mouth as she screamed and yanked her into the shadows.

Jake lay unconscious on the ground at her feet.

Oh, Jake! Lord, please let him be alive!

"That's what he gets for trying to protect you," a man whispered in her ear, his iron grip still in place.

Kelsey squeezed her eyes shut, tears streaming from the corners. "Just take the boat and leave us alone."

"The boat? We don't want the boat."

"What then?" Kelsey choked out the question.

"What else? What you smuggled into the country on *The Buccaneer.*"

FOUR

"What I smu—"

Hard and crushing, his hand clamped over her mouth again, cutting off her words.

"Quiet. Someone's coming." His whisper in her ear was barely audible, but the menace in his tone unmistakable.

All the more reason to make noise.

Kelsey screamed as loud as she could even though her muffled voice wouldn't go far. She kicked and thrashed, knocking them both into the wall behind them. Hearing his unexpected grunt brought a measure of satisfaction, but it wasn't enough. It didn't keep him from carrying her deeper into the shadows like she was nothing more than a rag doll.

She caught a glimpse of another man behind her. He was big and burly like a lumberjack and lifted Jake's dead weight over his shoulder in a fireman's carry with ease. How would they ever escape these men? She squeezed her eyes shut as if that would somehow give her more strength and bucked against her captor's harsh grip. It didn't faze him other than to annoy him. She was nothing more than a gnat.

A panic like she'd never known engulfed her.

Behind the building, what looked like a commercial utility van, covered in gray paint primer, stood in their path and seemed the likely destination. Another guy jumped out of the van. This one was tall and lanky. His silver hair was slicked back into a long ponytail, which somehow fit with his round John Lennon glasses.

He ran around to open the double doors in the back of the vehicle.

She couldn't let these guys take them like this.

Jake. Wake up!

Forget that when he was awake he'd been powerless to stop any of this from happening. And that he certainly couldn't hear the screams in her mind.

She almost regretted not running across the street to the sheriff's office. Almost. She hadn't been able to leave Jake behind after she'd seen the threat on his life, but now she doubted either of them would see the end of the day.

"I don't know anything about a smuggled item." She forced the words out, hissing them against his palm, but her kidnapper wasn't interested in hearing the truth even if he could understand what she'd said.

He practically threw her into the rear of the cargo van, devoid of backseats, where she toppled onto the rubber-padded floorboard, pain searing her shoulder.

She screamed like her life depended on it because it did. Jake's life, too.

This could be her last chance. Arms pinned her down as Brawny—the man who'd carried her to the van—slapped duct tape over her mouth, silencing her cry for help. Had anyone heard her?

Probably not, considering Brawny had made quick work of silencing her. He was also fast to pin her fighting arms behind her. Compared to him, it was like she had no strength at all. Wrapping something hard and tight around her wrists, he finished off by securing her feet, too, with what she now saw were plastic ties. She wasn't likely to escape those.

The walls of the van, coupled with being gagged and bound, created a keen sense of claustrophobia. Anxiety spiked through her, as she watched helplessly while the men gagged and bound Jake.

And yet, in an odd way, the fact they were securing Jake, too, gave her a surge of hope. That meant Jake was still alive and they expected him to recover enough to be a threat if he wasn't restrained. Though not much, it was something, and Kelsey took heart in that, her relief a powerful force that she used to keep from crumpling under the weight of this nightmare.

The van spun from its hiding place behind the building and bumped along the back roads. Kelsey closed her eyes and concentrated, paying attention to the stops and to the right or left turns. She had no way of knowing if her sense of where they were headed would help her. But the island was small enough that if she somehow managed to escape, knowing where she was or how to make her way back to the county sheriff's substation was important. The quicker they could get help, the better.

Regrettably she and Jake had spent too much time arguing to realize they had been followed. Though neither of them had voiced it, she realized now that they'd relied on the false sense of security offered by being in town where they were surrounded by people. If they were going to survive, she'd need to stay calm and stay focused on the route to safety.

It was strange, though, that these men hadn't been reluctant to grab them so near the sheriff's office. That struck her as crazy if not odd.

It could only mean whatever they were after was worth the risk.

Brawny sat on the floor across from her and held on to a hand grip against the interior wall, staring down at her. She eyed him back, willing him to understand her. *I don't know anything about what you're looking for!*

The problem was he didn't have that intelligent look in his dull eyes and soon gave up watching her as if bored. This whole thing was a big mistake. But how could she convey that to the man with tape over her mouth? What was worse, now that she and Jake were captives, they were also liabilities. They had seen the men's faces. That alone sealed their fate.

She figured Brawny wasn't the man she needed to convince of this colossal mistake, anyway. Hoping to get a better look at the guy in the driver's seat, she angled her head. She figured he was the man she needed to persuade if she even got the chance.

The van stopped abruptly, jolting Kelsey so that she rolled forward and her face pressed into the dirty mat that smelled of grease and fish. Familiar sounds resounded around her. Boats powering up or parking in slips, revving in the distance. Too many seagulls vying for food.

The marina.

The storm had subsided and a little rain wouldn't stop people from going about their business in this part of the world—they learned to live with it.

But stopping at the marina had to mean the men planned to sneak her and Jake onto a boat, likely *The Buccaneer,* to either search for what they were after, or…take them out to sea and dump them overboard. A shiver ran along her already wet and chilled skin.

Kelsey still had fight left in her, and she wouldn't make it easy for them to get her out of this van and onto the boat. This would be her chance to make someone take notice. Hopefully that person would succeed in contacting the sheriff where she and Jake had failed. But she didn't have time to berate herself more than she already had.

All three men left her alone in the van with Jake. Strange. Standing outside, they discussed their plans but she couldn't understand what they said. Were they making this up as they went? Who were these guys?

And who had smuggled something onto *The Buccaneer?* Captain Neely and his wife? That scenario didn't seem likely, but neither could Kelsey imagine Davis involved. One thing she knew for sure, she hadn't been the smuggler, but she almost wished she had, that way she could give the jerks what they wanted and be done. It almost seemed worse to be inadvertently caught in the middle of someone else's smuggling operation.

Regardless, these guys had gotten their information all wrong. The smuggled item must be seriously valuable for the men to go to this kind of trouble—shooting at her and Jake and then chasing them on speedboats. In the end, perhaps they would even commit murder if they hadn't already.

Her spine bristled.

If these were her last few minutes to live... *Oh, please, dear God, let it not be so.*

She'd made a mess of so much. Left others undone. She'd hoped to do more with her life.

What might she have done differently? Most of what she'd done over the past few months had been dictated by everything that had gone wrong in her relationship with Jake. And everything that had gone wrong with him had been dictated by her father's adulterous actions and her reaction to them. The whole thing, a domino effect.

But Jake claimed to be different. Maybe he was and Kelsey was too blind to see until it was too late.

To look at him now, hurt and unconscious... *Oh, Jake...*

Kelsey wriggled her way closer to where he lay.

She wanted to whisper his name, but her mouth was taped shut and her dry throat was beyond tired from screaming. Blood caked his hair on the side of his head. What had they hit him with? He might have a concussion. It was a bad sign that he was unconscious. She prayed he would wake up. If only she could have the past year to do over again. Where would she be now? Where would *they* be now?

Together?

Safe?

At the thought and all the memories—at least the good ones—Kelsey's heart warmed and broke at the same time. What she wouldn't give to have another chance with him.

The fact that she wished for another chance...did that mean she still loved him?

Kelsey caught her errant thoughts and heart, reining them in. She obviously wasn't thinking clearly and had fallen victim to fear and exhaustion.

Silence, except for the typical sounds of a busy dock, tugged her from her tumultuous thoughts and back to the current predicament. She could no longer hear the men's voices outside the van. Were they stupid enough to leave her here unguarded?

With every intention of taking advantage of the reprieve they'd inadvertently been given, she maneuvered her way toward the back and positioned her legs for kicking through the door, pulling them back like she would on a leg press machine and angling them to launch a hard kick against the door.

She thrust her feet forward and pounded hard, repeating the process.

Come on, give a little, would you?

Even if the door wouldn't budge, maybe someone passing the van would hear the noise and investigate.

The next time she hurled her legs forward, she met nothing but air when the double doors swung out. A dark blanket filled the space where the doors had been and fell on her body and face, wooly and itchy. Kelsey fought, twisting and kicking, as someone wrapped her in the scratchy blanket, but it was no use. She was hefted from the van and efficiently tucked into a small, cramped space.

A wooden crate? Like someone would use to store produce? So this was how they planned to get her onto the boat— she was nothing more than a few bags of potatoes.

"No!" she screamed against the tape.

Her heart raced, but she stopped thrashing. Working herself

into a frenzy wasn't helping at all. If anything, she couldn't get enough air.

She willed her rising anxiety to stop by imagining open spaces instead of the freakishly small one they'd folded her into. Otherwise she just might go crazy.

Lord, please, don't let my life end like this. Don't let Jake die. Help us out of this. Show us a way. Be my Guiding Light!

The crate shifted and so did she as they lifted it from the ground. Kelsey forced her breathing to slow even as her pulse jumped to her throat. Would they do the same to Jake? And how long would she have to stay in this crate?

She remained calm and still as the men transferred her to what she presumed was a boat. As she rested on her side, tears streaked across her eyes and over the bridge of her nose onto the blanket. She couldn't fight her captors anymore and wanted them to know she was ready to cooperate.

But how could she tell them? And how would she cooperate?

A deep, aching throb split across the darkness.

Jake stirred, awareness slowly anchoring his chaotic thoughts and distorted images to the surroundings. He had to be waking from a bad dream. One in which someone had hammered his head with a heavy mallet.

Opening his eyes, he found himself on his side, his face pressed against a taupe leather seat in the galley of a boat.

The Buccaneer?

That accounted for the distinct rolling sense of movement. Or maybe that was his gut's response to his headache. And where was he being taken?

Hands tied behind his back, he tried to right himself. He pushed with his legs and discovered his ankles were shackled, as well. Duct tape covered his mouth. Realizing he wasn't alone, he jerked his head to the side, shards of pain rewarding him.

Across the cherry dining table from him on the wrap-around sofa, Kelsey watched, her mouth covered in duct tape, too.

Kelsey! His heart fought to escape his chest.

Her features haggard, concern and fear poured from her eyes along with the tears, but if he was reading her right they were tears of relief mixed with joy.

Kelsey... He tried to communicate his anguish through his gaze, wishing she could read his mind, but maybe she didn't have to, considering the obvious unfavorable circumstances—his distress reflected her own. And so did his relief at seeing her.

Still...

If she wasn't here with him now, maybe she could have been somewhere safe. How could he have let this happen to her? He slipped his lids closed and tried to recall what had happened. He'd been following Kelsey, frustrated and arguing with her about their disenchanted past. The sheriff's sub-station was ahead of them, less than twenty-five yards away.

Twenty-five yards!

The men had been interested in much more than the boat or they wouldn't have pursued Kelsey and Jake within ear-shot of the law.

Kelsey had disappeared from his line of sight when someone grabbed him from the back and dragged him behind a building. Before he could react, he felt the sharp edge of a knife pressed against his throat. Felt the trickle of hot blood mingle with rain against his skin. If only he'd taken the risk to his life when he'd needed to in order to save her from this.

If only he'd been willing to make that sacrifice.

Still, why hadn't she run to the sheriff? He'd willed her to run with his eyes—she'd read him then, he *knew* she had. He'd seen the contemplation in her face—she'd considered running for help. But no. She'd been the one to sacrifice.

For him. But why?

The question burning through his mind, he opened his eyes and stared at her. He gritted his teeth, hating the way she watched him now. Her expression turned grim and she looked away. She must be reading his frustration at her for not closing the distance to the sheriff's office.

As soon as she looked away, he regretted showing her his displeasure. What was he thinking by getting angry with her like this? It wasn't really her—it was the whole crazy predicament he was angry with. And himself for not paying more attention. For not getting them to safety in time. Neither one of his brothers would have allowed this to happen. They always called Jake MIA—missing in action.

He was never there when it counted. He'd tried to be when it came to his relationship with Kelsey, not that it had mattered in the end. As for today, he might as well have been MIA because he'd not come through when it had really counted.

This was in no way Kelsey's fault. But... *You should have run, Kelsey. You should have run.*

Jake wasn't worth the sacrifice she'd made. Didn't she know that?

As his gaze roamed over her exhausted face and rumpled clothes, bile rose in his throat at the thought of what she'd been through. They'd been abducted, *The Buccaneer* hijacked.

The yacht might as well have been hijacked with them on board to begin with, for all the good their temporary escape had done them. How long would it take his brother Connor to figure out something was wrong, and then to find them? Kelsey's gaze drifted back to Jake's. She was counting on him. He forced his expression to warm—the only way he knew to reassure her. He wasn't good for much else, but he was good for that.

He knew when his attempt was working because her gaze softened. She'd always had the biggest, most beautiful eyes with that slight Asian slant, and they watched him now, wide and battle weary, despite his silent reassurance. For all the quarreling they'd done over what now seemed like trivial matters, he almost wondered if God wasn't playing a joke on them—here they were with their harsh words stifled, and left with only their gazes to communicate, to console each other.

There was a message in there somewhere, he was sure of it. *Fair enough, God. Fair enough.*

The vessel heaved a little too much for comfort, and Jake was grateful for the table keeping the both of them in place. With a groan, Kelsey leaned forward and pressed her forehead against the cherrywood.

All Jake wanted to do was reach over and hold her.

Someone clunked down the steps from above deck and entered the luxurious galley, his seething eyes locking with Jake's. Jake recognized the man who'd held the knife at his throat. When he'd been tugged behind the building again, fearing in his gut that Kelsey wouldn't run, that's when he'd taken the chance.

Too little. Too late.

He'd elbowed the man in the gut, receiving a surface scratch across his neck, and turned to fight. Everything had gone dark then. Obviously someone else had ambushed Jake from behind, knocking him unconscious.

And that explained the thundering in his head.

The guy was definitely a bodybuilder with a few facial scars bearing witness to his affinity for a good fight. Crossing his arms, he stood in a wide stance, eyeing Jake and Kelsey. He stepped near Kelsey and Jake's pulse ratcheted up, fearing what the man might do. He ripped the tape from Kelsey and she grimaced.

Jake didn't flinch when the guy ripped the tape from his mouth. Instead he glared. He wanted to sling a few choice words hoping they could do some damage, but he wouldn't risk more harm to Kelsey.

"Sorry about this, but we couldn't have you running to the sheriff, could we?"

He's sorry? Unbelievable. "What do you want with us?" Jake asked.

"They think I've smuggled something onto *The Buccaneer*," Kelsey offered.

Wait. Kelsey wouldn't do something like that. No way. "What?" Jake glowered at the man. Oh, how he'd love to squeeze the guy's throat, and not just because of his accusation.

"I don't think. I know. And every minute you hold out on us our profits go down significantly."

Us? Who were these guys?

"Listen to me. Try to understand." Kelsey dragged the words out slowly. "Why would I run to the sheriff if I had smuggled something?"

Good one. Jake almost wanted to clap for emphasis. Maybe he would have if his hands had not been tied behind his back.

The man's face went blank. She had him there.

"Because you don't have the good sense to know better. How should I know? But here's what I do know." The guy whipped out a cell phone.

Jake's cell phone.

His heart clamored against his ribs. If Connor couldn't get a hold of Jake, he'd know something was up. He'd come himself to make sure nothing was wrong or send for help. They'd worked out a plan in case the worst happened. And the worst had definitely happened.

Please, God.

Kelsey, on the other hand, was on a travel writing assignment. Was there anyone expecting her return on a certain day?

"A man named Connor left a text for you. He wanted to know when you were going to deliver the package."

Jake stared at the angular-faced bully, finally comprehending the inference.

"The package is this boat, you idiot," Jake said. "*The Buccaneer.* I'm a…repo man."

The guy laughed and hard. That was the one thing Jake hated about his job—saying he was a repo man didn't impress people as much as when he could say he was a commercial pilot. The job title wasn't nearly as elegant. People never looked at him the same way.

"Well, repo man. This is what we're gonna do. I'm going to call back this contact, and you're going to tell him you'll be out of reach for a few days."

Fury burned the back of Jake's throat. "I'm not telling him anything," he hissed.

The guy slid into the seat next to Kelsey and wrapped his massive arm around her neck. He stared at Jake while he tightened his hold. Jake knew he could crush her throat with his bare hands. She winced, but didn't cry out.

"Okay," Jake said. "Okay."

"That's better. Now, let's go over this again. I'm returning this call." The guy paused, glanced at Kelsey and grinned. "In fact, let's make it a little more interesting. Tell him you met someone so he shouldn't call you again. You'll get back to him in a few days. The girl's life for a little white lie. Do we have an agreement?"

Jake nodded, hating the thick knot that expanded in his throat and strangled him. He had to sound convincing, or Kelsey would pay the price. But how to clue Connor in without this guy knowing, too, and then hurting Kelsey, Jake didn't know.

Sweat trickled down his back. He squeezed his eyes shut and took a few deep breaths. The phone was already connecting as the man held it to Jake's face.

Connor answered. "*Where* have you been? You need to call me and let me know what's going on—"

"Connor!" Jake started out a little too harsh and steadied his voice. "Look, I'm sorry about that. I…I met someone."

"You *met* someone? What does that have to do with anything? Okay... Who is she?"

Jake hated that condescending tone. He'd worked hard to convince his brother—just like Kelsey—that he'd changed. He didn't want to give him another reason to think of Jake as MIA. But Connor's tone said as much, telling Jake that Connor thought he was acting out the old Jake who would disappear for days with someone he just met. Might as well play it like that. "Just...somebody I used to know."

He kept his eyes closed not daring to look at her. He desperately wanted to say more than that, but this just wasn't the time, the place...or even the way.

"Do you have the boat or not? Wait. Don't tell me... You are *not* taking the boat cruising with this girl, are you?"

In a way that was the truth. "No, I'm not. I need a few days off, so don't worry about me. I'll call you."

"But, Ja—"

A thick finger ended the call, and to Jake's unfathomable relief, the guy moved away from Kelsey to stand. Her eyes glistened with unshed tears as she stared at Jake. She blinked them away.

"And as for you," he directed his words at Kelsey, "nobody has called. No one will even miss you." He shook his head, mock pity in his eyes.

"Whatever it is you're after has to be something that Captain Neely took. We're not involved," she said. "So you can let us go."

"Can't you see she's telling the truth?" Jake asked. "You made a mistake when you took us. Neely's the guy to ask." What was he saying? He had no idea what they were after or if Neely was their man. Nor did he want to know—that would only sink the knife deeper into his and Kelsey's fate.

"What is it you think that I smuggled?" she asked.

Don't go there, Kelsey! Jake ground his molars. The less they knew the better.

"I'm not buying your little act, so you can stop."

"Did you search the boat? If Neely smuggled something on *The Buccaneer* then it might still be here."

The guy swiped his hand down his face like he'd grown seriously impatient. "Of course, we looked already. It's not here, unless we missed something. That's why we need you."

For the first time, Jake noticed a few cabinets askew, but the men hadn't ripped the walls open and the seat cushions were still intact. And a laptop rested on a kitchen counter— Kelsey's or Neely's?

"As for Neely, he's dead now. That leaves you. I'll give you time to think on that. But don't take too long." The man turned his back on them and disappeared up the stairs.

At the news, Jake shut his eyes. He couldn't even look at Kelsey for fear she'd see the hopelessness there. Their captors refused to believe they knew nothing about the smuggling and his brother thought he was off on a joyride with an old girl-friend. Jake sank deeper into the seat, feeling like all was lost.

Neely was dead. They were being taken who-knew-where. He'd been afraid to ask about Neely's wife, but the guy didn't mention her, so maybe that was a good thing. Maybe she got away, and *she* would be the one to send help, to tell the police, and they could hope on that.

But if Neely's wife were involved in the smuggling, maybe she wouldn't go to the police with the news of her husband's murder. Jake couldn't count on any help.

If he and Kelsey didn't find a way out of this and quickly, they were both going to die.

FIVE

"You sure you don't know what they're after?" he asked, a careful edge to his tone.

"How could you accuse me of smuggling something? Even if I had, you think I'd risk both our lives by refusing to tell them where it is? I would turn it over to them if I had it."

"That's not what I meant." This time, regret softened his voice.

His head was still caked with blood from his wound. A few new creases lined his forehead, and his amazing blue eyes had turned a little bloodshot. That coupled with his rugged, unshaven jaw made him look far more haggard than she'd ever seen, and still the guy could turn her head if he'd been a stranger she'd passed on the street. Or maybe that wasn't it at all—maybe he only looked good to her no matter what. She couldn't see him the way someone else might see him because Kelsey had a history with this man. She had feelings for him she hadn't been able to leave behind, and those feelings were swirling to the surface and coloring everything that was happening now.

She hated that she'd snapped at him. He was tired and worn, just like she was. "I'm sorry. This whole thing has me frazzled."

Pressing her head against the cream-colored wall behind her, she shut her eyes. If she tried really hard, she might be able to imagine this was just another day like so many she'd had on *The Buccaneer.* She envisioned herself sitting at the table working on her articles for the magazine, or browsing through the images she'd taken of the San Juan Islands. But the discomfort, her bound arms and legs, wouldn't let her mind drift, and she couldn't shake the sense of Jake's presence across from her. That alone kept her anchored to the moment.

"Besides, even if I *did* know," she finally said, "telling them now wouldn't give us much opportunity to live. They'd just kill us once they got what they wanted. We need a bargaining chip."

Jake didn't reply, at first, then, "I didn't want to know what they're after. I guess I was hanging on to that last shred of hope that if we didn't know anything, they'd let us go." He exhaled, long and hard. "But it doesn't sound like they're going to believe us. Or let us go. You're right—our only chance of living now is to find what they want. That's our negotiating tool."

Kelsey peered at him from beneath heavy lids. "Have you heard a word I've said? I *don't* know what they're after."

"Think." He emphasized the word like she wasn't already racking her brain. "Since you've been on the boat and with Neely, you might have overheard something. Maybe we can figure things out."

"And then what?"

"Bargain with the information. Escape. Any number of scenarios comes to mind. Knowing nothing isn't going to work in our favor."

...*work in our favor*... He'd said those same words about the weather on the beach when they'd first met. The reminder finally succeeded in sending her mind back to another time and place. An image flitted through her thoughts. She and Jake sitting on the beach in Maui. They'd talked and talked, never running out of things to say. Like they had everything in common and all the time in the world. She wished for that now. By the end of that day, she'd wanted to run her hands through his thick, dark hair, but it had been another week before she'd followed through. Here they were in a completely different situation—no beach or sunshine or freedom, and running out of time. And instead of being filled with anticipation and the excitement that had come with a new relationship, resentment simmered under the surface.

"What if I just made something up?" she asked. "Say I know where it is, but we have to go ashore to find it?"

Yes, it would be a lie, but wouldn't God understand the dire circumstances? Wouldn't He understand they needed to escape?

Jake shot her a warning frown. "No, that's too dangerous. I don't want you digging yourself in deeper. I'll do the talking."

His tone was a little too condescending if you asked her. "Are you for real?"

"Listen, Kelsey, you keep taking what I say the wrong way. Maybe I'm not communicating well. But we're on the same team here, okay? We have to work together. I'm trying to protect you."

"For your information, I don't need your protection." Why count on men? *They only cheat on you and leave you.*

"What's wrong with me wanting to keep you from getting hurt?" Pain reflected behind his eyes.

"You didn't seem to care about that before." Oh…why had she said that? It didn't even apply to their current situation—all her emotions were getting tangled up and she struggled to separate what was happening now with what happened before.

Their problems of the past needed to stay there, at least until they figured out how to survive. She knew that logically, yet she couldn't have a conversation with Jake, or even be in the same room with him, without all the hurt and bitterness resurfacing. At this point, she wasn't sure the derogatory feelings were directed at him. She was the one with the insurmountable issues.

Pathetic. She hadn't realized how much of the hurt she'd held on to until seeing him.

"I can't stand by and watch you get hurt," he said. "I realize now that I shouldn't have counted on you to run to the sheriff. I should have turned and fought the guy holding that knife to my throat the instant it happened. Then you wouldn't be here."

That moment played across her mind now, the moment she'd had to choose between safety and losing Jake. "I…I couldn't leave you, Jake. I couldn't let them kill you."

Maybe things would be different now if she had crossed the street and gotten help. Yeah. And maybe Jake would be dead. Two men came down the steps and put an end to her issues of the heart, and whatever escape plans she and Jake could have made.

Brawny and the hippie faced them. The tall man with the ponytail looked like a thinker; he had that intelligent way about him. Kelsey had decided from the beginning he was the man in charge, but he didn't brandish a weapon.

No. He left that to Brawny who flashed a nine-millimeter for good measure.

After adjusting his John Lennon glasses, he crossed his arms. "You claim you don't know anything."

Was it a statement or a question? Or did the guy just want confirmation?

"We're telling the truth," Jake said. "And if it's all the same to you, we don't want to know anything. We don't want to learn what you're after. That way you can just let us off at the nearest marina and be on your way, and we have nothing to tell anyone."

Kelsey eyed Jake, confused that he'd reverted to his initial plan, but she supposed the truth was worth one last try.

The man squinted, studying Jake. "I like the way you think. Were I in your shoes, I might have said the same thing. But it's not going to work that way this time."

He lost interest in Jake and his gaze traveled to Kelsey.

"Cut them free." He directed his words to Brawny and Brawny's partner who'd trailed them into the galley.

He wore a patch over his eye. She hadn't noticed that before. They were modern-day pirates, it seemed, after missing loot.

Brawny made quick work of cutting the plastic ties from her wrists and ankles, and Jake's, as well. Kelsey wasn't sure if this was a good thing or not. She had no idea what to expect. Jake scooted closer to her and, pressing his hand over hers, he squeezed. She'd lied when she had said she didn't want or need his protection. She wanted protection, but not if it meant he would get hurt. How could he protect her and deflect harm to himself?

Lord, what are we going to do?

"An old and rare map, oh, about this size—" Lennon held his hands apart just under a foot "—doesn't ring a bell?"

His voice not a little sarcastic, Kelsey almost failed at stifling her scoff. This was like some sort of Robert Louis Stevenson pirate story. "Don't tell me—a treasure map?"

Lennon's shoulders shook with silent laughter. "Not at all. The map *itself* is the treasure, considering what collectors are willing to pay. Or at least, one collector in particular. Neely's had this operation going for years. Smuggling maps and books and the like to collectors. Black-market antiquities. Stuff from museums. And you're telling me you didn't know anything about it?"

A sense of hope ignited, mingling with her desperation. Could she convince him to let them go? "I promise you, I was just a passenger hired to finish out a travel writing assignment for someone else. Please, just let us go."

"I happen to know from a reliable source that passengers aboard *The Buccaneer* are handpicked. Have you ever considered what the name means?" He studied her.

"Pirate," Jake said. "So what? That doesn't mean anything. People name their boats all sorts of things."

The man ignored Jake, his focus on Kelsey intensifying. "What I'm trying to say is that I'm not buying your act, love."

He took a step toward her, the malicious intent in his eyes surprising. His British accent didn't ring true. But he wasn't American, either. She hadn't seen him as the brutal type, using Brawny and his cohort to carry out violence. He started another step toward her, but in that moment, Jake bolted up and blocked his path.

My protector.

"Don't touch her," he said.

Lennon adjusted his glasses again. "I can see why you want to play the hero, win the girl, but again, that isn't going to work." He tugged what looked like Kelsey's shock gun from his back pocket and examined it like he might consider using it.

Jake stood his ground.

"All right, I'll play along." Lennon cleared his throat. "I shouldn't touch her, or what?"

"You'll have to go through me first."

Words of bravado with not much to back them up, that's all they were.

Jake didn't have a well-thought-out plan and all his moves were defensive and reactionary. But no way could he sit there and do nothing while this man threatened Kelsey.

The guy moved closer, his face mere centimeters from Jake's. He could almost swear the guy snarled—or maybe that was Jake. This man staring him down enjoyed this game far too much to be angry.

"I'm sure Flanagan was hoping you'd say that."

Flanagan? The bodybuilder on steroids behind this skinny pole of a man cracked his knuckles. Sometimes, the only move left to a guy was to throw himself in front of the train.

"Yeah? Why's that?" Jake asked, but he didn't have to. He understood Flanagan's kind. He understood the man wanted vengeance for what little pain Jake had inflicted on him back in town.

At least this time, with the wall to his back, Jake wouldn't get slammed in the head from behind again, which was good considering he wasn't sure his skull could take much more. At least this would be a fair fight. Fair fight or not, looking at the size of this guy, he wasn't sure his triathlon training would make much of a difference.

"Because Flanagan loves a good fight, and I love to watch." The man crossed his arms. "Let's see what you've got."

Did he expect Jake to punch him?

"Boys." The man stepped back and left Jake to face off with Flanagan and the other so-far nameless, one-eyed hulk. This wouldn't be a good fight.

This would be painful.

If Kelsey had any brains—and he knew she did—she'd make a run for it this time, while he had their attention. He glanced her way, not puffed up like a cock-fighting rooster, but to plead with her—he was buying her a chance.

But all she did was give a slight shake of her head in answer. She wouldn't run because she wouldn't leave him. And there was a matter of where would she go out in the middle of the Salish Sea. He didn't know how far they were from the islands or how far she could swim. For all Jake knew, they were in the Strait of Juan de Fuca heading out into the Pacific.

Jake Jacobson, you're an idiot.

But he did know one thing for certain—he couldn't back down now. He was free and had a chance to fight, and, in fact, a call to fight. What testosterone-driven man could deny the challenge?

"Jake." Her voice cracked. "Please don't do this now."

Her hand wrapped around his. He shrugged free.

And slammed his fist into Flanagan's gut. Pain engulfed his hand. Without so much as a flinch, Flanagan grinned, laughing at what had to look like a feeble attempt on Jake's part to hurt him.

Okay. New tactic here.

He drew on memories from his high school football days and thrust his shoulder into the other guy's diaphragm, pushed forward until the guy hit the wall, all while he shouted for Kelsey to run.

The reprieve he'd given her didn't last long. Flanagan yanked Jake off his partner and returned Jake's favors. Pain engulfed his stomach, then his face.

Payback.

A few more punches and Jake lay on the floor, gripping his bruised insides. He might as well have attempted to fight a rhinoceros.

"You've made a mistake." He forced the words through gritted teeth, unsure if they were even coherent. "We don't know anything."

Kelsey was by his side, begging them now. "No more, please! I'll try to remember something. Just give me some time. I'll help you find what you want, if you'll leave him alone."

"Okay, that's enough." The leader's words floated somewhere above Jake.

He'd responded to Kelsey's pleas. What was that about?

"We don't want him to end up like Neely. Not yet anyway."

Okay, maybe it wasn't so much Kelsey's pleas but the man's need to keep Jake alive for future use. Maybe he could use that. If Jake could somehow take down the one guy in charge, then maybe the others would leave them alone. Cut off the head of the snake, as it were. A plan to keep in mind for later, but right now, he'd do better to play along. Wait for the right moment to strike. The brutes grabbed him by the shoulders and biceps and lifted him to his feet. They shoved him into a room with a bed that took up half the space. Jake fell on the mattress, glad for the reprieve.

"Jake." Kelsey was at his side, tears in her voice. "I'm so sorry."

"What are you sorry—" Pain stabbed him, cutting off his words. "I'm the one who is sorry. I tried and failed you again. But next time I give you a chance, you have to take—"

"Shh. Just rest now." Her honey-sweet voice washed over him, and he soaked it up.

The next thing he knew, Kelsey ran a warm, wet cloth over his head and face, wiping away the grime and blood. He let her. He heard the rip of paper. The strong scent of an antiseptic accosted him before he felt the sting as she swabbed his cuts and bruises. She'd obviously found a first aid kit.

"What are we going to do, Lord?" Kelsey whispered softly.

Probably thought Jake hadn't heard. She seemed to think he'd passed out, succumbed to his wounds. He didn't want her to believe he was weak, but having her attention like this was priceless and he'd drift off willingly with her nurturing. But how much longer before the men returned to beat information out of him? Or worse, out of her? He winced at the thought.

Information that neither of them had. In a way this was reminiscent of his problems with Kelsey that had led to their breakup. She'd accused him of having an affair with another woman. She'd been furious that he wouldn't tell her what had happened, but how could he confess to her when what she wanted to hear was a lie to begin with? But now she was the one who wasn't believed when she tried to tell the truth. Jake slid one eye open to sneak a peek, but she caught him.

"Think there's a way to escape without having to fight our way out?" he asked.

Her gentle smile burned inside him, almost making him forget the pain. Still, he knew the curve in her lips was for his benefit, but fear and uncertainty lingered where her smile didn't reach. Another reminder of another day. Though he'd hated seeing those feelings in her eyes *then,* her life hadn't been on the line like it was *now.*

How could he save her when she failed to act on every chance he gave her?

SIX

The Buccaneer rocked, moving with the storm-driven waters, and Kelsey held on to the edge of the bed where she tended Jake. Before this, she'd not endured much in terms of turbulent waters—the Inside Passage had protected her from the rougher waters of the Pacific. Where was *The Buccaneer* headed now?

Kelsey glanced over at the door that remained half opened. From here, she could see the guy with the patch, sitting at the table laying down cards. *Solitaire?* Next to his stack of cards was a gun, and next to the gun, the electroshock device.

"Where do you think Lennon is taking us?" She whispered the question.

Jake rolled his head to the side and looked at her, pain still gripping his features. "Lennon?" He laughed a little. "I wish I knew."

A nasty cut at his temple bled through the bandage she'd taped over it so she replaced it. "Do you think we're headed to the Pacific? The water is rougher than before."

"I hope not." He swiped a hand down his face. "It's just the storm, I believe."

"That doesn't make me feel any better."

He shoved upright and threw his legs over the bed to sit next to her, wincing as he moved. "That's the least of our worries. In fact, we could have a better chance of surviving…"

The look in his eyes told her he regretted his words. "Come here," he said and lifted his arm in invitation like he'd done when they had stood under the awning while it rained.

That seemed like a lifetime ago, and yet it had only been a few hours.

Kelsey didn't want Jake risking himself for her. Nor did she want to give him the impression that she needed him to comfort and reassure her. And yet, being with him now, she felt like she was back where she'd been a year ago, when it had broken her heart to walk away from him.

She stood, moving away from him. On shaky legs she made her way to the porthole to look outside, leaving him to watch her go. Frowning, he lay back down on the bed. She had to put distance between them. That had been her reason a year ago when they'd split.

Distance would bring clarity—give her time to think on whether or not to believe him about what happened. Whether or not she could trust him. Distance was supposed to make things easier. Instead, she'd missed him terribly, and yet, she hadn't bothered to call him. Nor had he called her. She'd taken a small step away and kept walking, and before she knew it she was too far from him to find her way back even if Heather didn't stand between them.

But in Kelsey's mind, Heather was still there, leaving Jake's apartment. Maybe Jake had told her the truth when she'd accused him of cheating. Her voice during their argument rang in her ears now, and she sounded like her mother accusing her father. For years, the woman had looked the other way when it came to his cheating until finally she had ended their twenty-five-year marriage, giving Kelsey a healthy dose of fear of love and commitment.

That evening, Jake had invited Kelsey over for a special dinner he was cooking himself. She had remembered the anticipation, and even the small hope that he might propose—

they'd grown so close. Were in love. Talked about their future together like it was a given.

She'd never been so devastated in her life than when she'd shown up a little early and watched another woman leave his apartment.

Never. She would never be like her mother and ignore the obvious. The hurt ached in her heart afresh, and Kelsey knew she would never get over that moment of betrayal. Then there was Jake, watching her, and she saw the hurt she'd caused him by walking out on their relationship in the past, by not believing and trusting him—it reflected in his eyes this moment.

She couldn't trust him then, and she wouldn't give in to her heart and trust him now—at least in a romantic relationship. She couldn't risk letting herself love him again. But in this horrible situation, he was the only one she could lean on. And she could hardly stand to see the pain in his eyes.

She focused her attention on the darkness, her only glimpse into the early night that had been ushered in by the storm, when lightning split open the sky.

"It's dark and stormy outside." She steadied herself by clinging to a sconce. "That sounded like dialogue from a B movie."

"Yeah, well, even B movies can have good endings," Jake said.

"You mean where the bad guys die and the good guys live?"

"And girls. Good guys and girls." Jake offered her a grin that sent her heart racing just like old times. Even in the middle of this nightmare. How'd he do that?

"But this isn't a movie," she murmured to herself. This was real life where the good guys died every day.

He pushed from the bed and, for a minute, Kelsey thought he would join her at the porthole. Instead he peeked through the half-open door.

"Figures," he whispered, "but I had to check."

With his incredibly toned physique, she wasn't sure just one of the men could keep him confined to his room. But the others had to be somewhere nearby. There weren't a lot of places for them to be on this boat though it was a decent size. Jake might overcome the one guy playing cards—that is, if the guard didn't have a chance to grab his weapon—but that would just leave him to face another man with freakishly large muscles.

No.

Jake and Kelsey had to come up with something else if they didn't want to remain captives. And even without their captors, they would still face the stormy sea. That's why the bad guys weren't worried at all that Kelsey and Jake would escape.

Still, why would they take *The Buccaneer* out during the storm and face rough waters? "Where are they heading that's so urgent we have to be on the water now?"

"To the person who really wants this map. Remember the man you called Lennon mentioned it was worth a lot to one particular collector. Could be Lennon wants to deliver it in Neely's place and collect the money. Or maybe he wanted to get it from Neely for a completely different collector. Who knows?" Jake paced the small space of the cabin. "The problem is that he still doesn't have it and thinks we can help him. Kelsey, we need a weapon. You don't happen to know where there's one stashed, do you?"

"You saw the one I had. I almost zapped you with it."

Jake snorted a laugh. "And I'm guessing that was yours that Lennon pulled from his pocket."

"Could be. He probably found it when they came aboard. I lost it during our first mad getaway." She was still hoping for a second.

"I wish you hadn't protected me by telling them you would help." He stopped pacing long enough to send her a warning look. "I don't want you making any commitments like that, especially on my behalf. Understand?"

"A simple thank-you would have been nice," she said and continued to stare out the porthole.

She felt a gentle squeeze to her shoulder. "You're right," he said, his whisper warming her. "Thank you."

Kelsey bit her lip, tugging on it, holding her emotions inside. When she didn't respond, Jake started pacing again— he had good sea legs compared to her. She didn't think she could stand too long if she wasn't holding on to something. But the storm would end sooner or later, and these men had chosen to ride it out for whatever reason.

"That brings us full circle," he said. "Spending time on this yacht with Neely and his wife, you could have overheard something. Can you remember anything Neely might have said about the map?"

She closed her eyes and tried to think things through, but it was no use. Her mind was clouded with fear. She shook her head and opened her eyes to see Jake watching her. "I'm sorry," she said.

"What about Burroughs? Your boss. This is his boat. I'd wager he's involved. Think about what Lennon said. Passengers on *The Buccaneer* are handpicked. Why would he choose you for this travel writing assignment?"

Kelsey pressed her fingertips against her temples. "This is just crazy. Davis is not only my boss, he's a great friend. Why would he get involved with something like this?"

Jake stared at her, and she had the feeling he was thinking the same thing she was. Davis was obviously struggling financially if Jake was sent to reclaim the boat for the bank. Had he taken to smuggling to restore his finances? She shook her head again, unable or unwilling to think the worst. "He's not a criminal. I won't believe it."

"I know it's hard to consider the possibility. But it's no more outrageous than the fact that *The Buccaneer* has been hijacked and we're on it together. This is happening. It's real. Whether you believe it or not, Burroughs could very well be involved. Now you have to get past any reservations and think. We need something to go on."

She was thinking all right. Nausea swirled in her stomach. "I think I'm going to be sick."

Jake was at her side. He gripped her arms and steadied her, his hands warm and reassuring. "You need to lie down. Is there anything on board for motion sickness?"

She nodded. "Check the cabinet in the bathroom."

She felt like such an idiot. A weakling. Jake was the one hurting. He was the one who needed medical attention.

He assisted her to the small bed that she'd used for the past few weeks. He disappeared into the bathroom and soon reappeared with a glass of water and a pill. She took it and drank the water. "Thanks."

"According to the label, you should have taken it before stepping on the boat, before you got sick. Have you used it before?"

"I haven't needed to, no." She wasn't sure if her problem was the rolling and rocking of the boat or the danger to their lives. Maybe a little of both. "Plus, it supposedly makes you drowsy and I didn't want to waste unnecessary time sleeping."

She curled up in a ball, wanting nothing more now than to fall asleep and then wake up from this nightmare.

Davis isn't involved. He can't be.

This was all a mistake. But Neely... She'd always felt a little uncomfortable around Neely and his wife. What happened to his wife anyway? The men hadn't mentioned anything about her, and Kelsey had been afraid to bring her up in case the men hadn't even known she existed. Had she escaped unnoticed? And if so, would she call the police and send help? Or was she dead, as well?

Unfortunately, no one would miss Kelsey for days except maybe Davis. *Oh, God, please let him not be involved. Please let him call the police because his boat is missing.*

Or because Kelsey hadn't called him to report on the trip.

Still, it was the weekend, and Davis wouldn't expect to hear from her yet. If only Neely hadn't convinced her to stay over an extra day on the islands before returning to Washington.

Her stomach roiled as her spirit sank deeper. Jake moved to sit next to her then hesitated, remaining upright. She'd love to know what he was thinking.

"You should get some rest," he said. "You're tired and maybe if you've rested, you'll remember something that will help us."

Not likely. Why was this happening to her? To them?

"But what about you?" she asked. "You're the one they hurt."

Twice now. First when they hit him over the head near the sheriff's substation.

"I'll be fine." He glanced at the sleeper chair in the corner. But Kelsey doubted he had any intention of sleeping. Likely he'd stand guard all night long, in addition to the sentinel bully already watching them.

Another wave of nausea hit her. She squeezed her eyes shut and curled tighter into the fetal position. "Jake," she whispered.

"I'm right here." His voice near, his soft shadow fell over her.

"When do you think they'll come for us again? I mean…"

"Not until the storm's over. Sleep now. You need your strength and all your wits for whatever's to come."

"I should be taking care of you."

"You already did, Kelsey."

"You already did," he whispered again so softly, she almost didn't hear.

Her tender touch had meant the world to him when it shouldn't.

Part of him wanted her attention. For her to feel something for him. He could see in her eyes and sense in her touch that she still cared, but with all that was in him, he had to fight that urge to slip back into old feelings. Recovering from losing the woman he loved—the woman he'd intended to propose to the night things had fallen apart—had been a long and hard road. He didn't relish going through that again, ever.

He stared down at her now. Seeing her looking so tired and vulnerable roused every protective instinct in spite of himself.

Jake was tempted to run his palm over her hair. Wanting to soothe her, he lifted his hand but hesitated before making contact. Though her eyes were closed, she subtly winced, like she didn't want to feel his touch. Like she'd somehow *known* he was reaching for her.

That hurt. He withdrew his hand and headed for the chair, reminding himself not to read too much into her actions. More than likely she was simply trying to gain control over the motion sickness, over her thoughts and emotions. The same as Jake. Her pained expression had nothing at all to do with him. He'd keep telling himself that.

And even if it had, why would it hurt him? He shouldn't feel anything for her in that way.

Right.

What am I doing? He couldn't think about this. He had to focus on getting them away from these men. He had every intention of seeing Kelsey out of this alive. Of both of them surviving this together.

But try as he might, his thoughts kept returning to the history he shared with Kelsey.

An overwhelming need to talk to her and say things they'd left unsaid warred with his better judgment. This could be his last chance. If he didn't live through this—because if anyone lived, he would make sure it was Kelsey—there were things he wanted her to know.

Things that weren't better left unsaid, after all. He saw that now. Funny how facing death could make a person want to say everything they kept in their hearts—all the deep, dark secrets.

She didn't know about his planned proposal. After her accusation and refusal to believe him, his pride had stood in the way from telling her what he'd intended. He wanted—no, needed—her to trust him without him having to prove himself at every turn.

They'd both lost their fathers in different ways. For different reasons. Kelsey's father was still alive, but she'd lost him when her parents had divorced, his affairs ruining her ability to trust anyone, especially men. Though Jake's father had died in a plane crash while in the Air Force, he'd left a huge hole in his family's life. Jake couldn't stand to watch how devastated his mother had been, not even counting his own pain at losing his father.

If he never loved anyone that much, never committed, Jake figured he could avoid that devastation. That plan had worked well until Kelsey had walked across his line of sight on that beach in Hawaii.

Once he'd gotten to know her, she'd changed everything. He'd been willing to take the risk of love and commitment with *her*. He just hadn't known losing her could happen the way it had. He'd lost her before he'd ever really had her.

But now? If he had to do it all over again, he would have proposed to her despite the way she'd hurt him. If he'd laid his heart out there and taken the risk of her trampling on it, maybe things would be different today.

And maybe, just maybe, he'd tell her everything when she woke up.

A gust of wind whistled through the porthole and the yacht swayed. The waters were a little rougher than he'd expect in the Salish Sea, even during a storm. Jake frowned at the thought. Where were they headed?

Like Kelsey, Jake couldn't imagine why they weren't sitting in a marina to ride out the storm, but maybe these men would rather face the storm than the authorities, considering that—if they'd told the truth—Neely was left dead at their hands. If Jake could believe anything they said.

Jake resettled himself in the chair. To say it was comfortable was pushing it. Watching the door, he felt like a guard dog, though he didn't have enough in his bite to do any real damage against the three of them. He couldn't even hold his own against Flanagan, as had already been proven.

He tried to ignore the storm that raged outside. He'd love to take the anti-motion sickness medicine, too, but he couldn't afford to lose his reaction time or get too groggy. Though he would rest, he would remain ready to jump up at an instant.

But with his muscles and neck knotted with tension, his body aching with bruises, the unending throbbing in his head and the constant awareness of the man guarding them just outside the room, he wasn't likely to fall asleep. Or so he thought.

When Jake woke up, having fallen asleep after all, he rubbed the crick in his neck—the result of the awkward position he'd slept in. The light that he'd left on was out. Had Kelsey turned it off?

The Buccaneer almost sat calmly in the water now, compared to the earlier ride. The storm had passed—either that or the men had pushed through it. They had to be running low on fuel, unless they had brought extra. When they stopped to refuel, Jake and Kelsey had to be ready to try to escape.

He wished there weren't so many unknown variables.

Moonlight spilled through the porthole. At least they'd made it through one storm—now to face another. He hoped the men wouldn't drag them out in the middle of the night to question them again.

In the dim light of the moonbeam that shined across the small room, he could see Kelsey's sleeping form. Earlier, he'd considered telling her everything. How much he'd loved her before, and maybe still did, and that he'd planned to propose. He didn't resist the memories of their time together, basking in the warmth that flooded his mind and heart, and even seemed to be a balm for his bruises, both physically and emotionally.

Obviously, Jake wasn't husband material for a girl like Kelsey, and on the other side of that romantic token, he couldn't let down his guard where she was concerned—she'd hurt him too much, and would hurt him again. Of that he had no doubt. But he wasn't asking her to consider a future with him—not now, when he didn't know if he'd live to see another day. He'd just like some closure.

Suddenly, her eyes fluttered open. "What are you thinking?" Her voice was soft and sleepy.

"Nothing." No, he wouldn't tell her. He had no way of knowing how she'd react. At the marina, their emotions had been too high to realize they were being followed. He couldn't risk such inattentiveness again.

Not when both their lives were on the line.

SEVEN

Gray morning light illuminated the stuffy room and sent dread through Kelsey. How long did she and Jake have before Lennon's attention turned to them again? What could they do to get free?

She scraped herself from the bed and headed to the bathroom. In the small lavatory, she examined her appearance in the mirror. The circles under her eyes and her pale face nearly made her gasp. Had it been just yesterday when she'd looked in the same mirror with a smile on her face, her day filled with hope and expectation? She'd planned to work on her travel articles and edit the pictures. She would probably have made one last foray onto the island.

But then the bullets had started, and Jake had appeared out of nowhere and had whisked her away. She'd thought he'd brought the trouble her way, but apparently, he was the one inadvertently caught in her nightmare involving *The Buccaneer*.

Now her face reflected the past twenty-four hours living in fear, and her hair wasn't any better. She splashed water on her skin and ran a brush through her hair as if how she looked mattered. Danger had a way of changing a person's perspective. But none of that changed the fact that she wanted to look good for Jake no matter the situation. That irked her. She shouldn't care if he thought she was attractive.

A noise in the room brought her thoughts back to the mo-

ment. She opened the door and stepped out to see Jake standing by the bedroom door in a defensive stance. He glanced
back at her and frowned. She could hear voices from the galley, a heated discussion.

Jake gestured for her to go back into the bathroom, but she
shook her head, refusing.

Lennon stepped into the room—his glasses looked a little crooked today. Jake backed away from him and stood in
front of her.

The man grinned. She hated that grin.

"Still trying to be the hero." He scrutinized Jake and then
his gaze moved to Kelsey like he'd decided Jake wasn't worth
his attention. "Did you come up with anything, love?"

"No," Jake said, pushing her completely behind him. "We
don't know anything. You're wasting your time."

*Jake, what are you doing? Convincing them we're a waste
of time could get us killed.*

The guy took a step toward Jake. "I'm pretty sure you
don't know anything, but *she* does. The only reason you're
still alive is because she cares about you. I can use you as
my leverage. I enjoyed watching how that worked last night."

Dear Lord, help us! Leaning her forehead against Jake's
back, Kelsey closed her eyes, nausea gripping her insides
again. But this time, the swirling sensation had nothing at
all to do with motion sickness.

"We're going to work on her memories today. I've planned
a day of fun-filled activities."

Jake's back tensed against her forehead. She couldn't take
this anymore. What if they planned to torture him with the
shock gun? She stepped from behind him. He thrust his arm
out to block her way.

"I can show you the article I was working on and the pictures I've taken," she said. "It's all on my laptop. It was right
there, on the kitchen counter. Maybe that will convince you

I don't know about this map. You can look through my computer and read my emails and then you'll see."

He grinned again. "All in good time. But I've already promised the boys a bit of fun. Ritter's a little anxious to pay your friend back for what he did last night."

Ritter must be the guy with the eye patch.

"Pay me back? Don't you think you've done enough already?"

Flanagan stepped through the door followed by Ritter wearing his eye patch, and they grabbed Jake.

At first, he resisted.

"Wait," Kelsey begged. "Please, tell me more. I can't help you unless I know more. How did you find out about this if you're not working with Neely? Who wants the map? I need to know more!" She screamed the last words as they dragged Jake through the galley until he disappeared up the stairs with the two of them. Lennon stayed behind and continued his insane grin, his arms crossed.

"You're enjoying this aren't you?" she asked.

"How could you tell?"

"What kind of sick person are you?" She hated the way her voice trembled, wishing she could stand strong against him.

"Sometimes a person is at the wrong place at the wrong time." He started across the galley without her. "But don't worry. This will be over sooner or later, and either you'll survive or you won't."

Kelsey stared after him, hanging on each malicious word.

He paused and looked back at her. "It doesn't work that well if you're not going to watch. You coming or what?"

Watch the men torture Jake? Did that mean she could help him by not following this cruel, insane person who cared more about a map than a human life? She thought about staying put, but decided against it. He was probably strong enough to drag her if she resisted, so what was the point.

Kelsey glanced around the galley and kitchen as she fol-

Riptide

lowed him. Neely. His wife. Where had they put the map? Was it even still on the boat? Had Neely already removed it? Where could it be? There were only so many places, and yet she could think of nothing that would help. All she came up with was a blank white canvas.

"Why don't you just tear the boat apart, piece by piece instead of keeping us here?" Instead of hurting them?

He paused on the steps and turned to face her. "Oh, believe me, we've looked. Maybe it's on the boat, maybe it's not. But if I sent these guys ripping through everything, we could inadvertently destroy the map and then it's worth nothing. *The Buccaneer's* worth a hefty sum, as well, as long as it remains intact. You understand why I can't just tear her up, right?"

"So instead you are hurting people. That's what I don't understand. Don't you think people are more valuable than an old map or a luxury yacht?"

Lines creased his forehead like she'd confused him. In his eyes, she was a stupid girl to ask such a question. Then his expression shifted to a thoughtful look. It scared her. His expression said he might decide she was worth something to him, but it wasn't the kind of look any woman wanted to see. Not from a man like him.

A shudder crawled over her and she rubbed her arms, looking away from his unwelcome gaze. Thank goodness, he decided to continue up the steps. She followed. What else could she do?

Above deck, Kelsey thought she would be sick again when she saw what they had planned for Jake.

Jake searched Kelsey's eyes as Ritter held him in place and Flanagan bound his wrists together with marine rope. Lennon… He just stood there behind Kelsey and watched.

The jerk.

Her face said it all—a torrent of tears spilled over her

cheeks. She shook her head, never taking her gaze from him. "Jake… I'm so sorry." Sobs choked her words.

Feeling completely helpless, he said nothing at all. But he couldn't leave her without saying at least something.

"It'll be okay," he finally said, but he didn't believe his own words. They were just all he could think to say. A person needed to have hope, no matter how small.

He would have tried to resist, to fight them, but he'd attempted fighting his way to freedom already and that hadn't worked. Besides, he was assured it was either him or her overboard. There was no way he could allow her to take his place.

They were going to throw him over the side and drag him. He drew in a breath. This could be the end of him.

He could drown. Or he could suffer with hypothermia and possibly freeze to death, depending on how long they left him—the water temperature had to be in the forties or low fifties.

But people swam here to train for triathlons, or to train for swimming the English Channel, that much he knew from his own training. With the thought, a tiny glow of hope kindled inside. Now he saw a reason for his insane need to throw himself into training for a triathlon race. A reason beyond his need to take his mind off losing Kelsey.

And that was going to pay off.

Head, guts, heart. That's what it took to get through a triathlon. Finally, he was using his head.

Because of his training, these guys would be hard-pressed to break him by dragging him behind the boat. At least, he'd be harder to break than someone without his experience. His captors didn't know his background and maybe he could use that to his advantage. Maybe if they thought they'd broken him, they would let down their guard.

He and Kelsey could escape. Or at least Kelsey could escape. He closed his eyes, sending a silent "thank You" to God for this one idea. Such a small thing and yet it could make all the difference.

His brothers had always said he was MIA, and Jake would wholeheartedly agree with them, but they couldn't understand how deep the truth went. He'd lost himself somewhere, lost the boy he had used to be—the guy who walked the straight and narrow. Who was on speaking terms with God. He'd simply lost his way after his father had died.

But right now, in this moment, Jake somehow *knew* that God was lighting the way back. But what he couldn't know, and no one could, was if finding himself again included finding a way out of this for him and Kelsey. He wouldn't worry about it for now.

He'd been given enough for the moment and would work with that.

Jake opened his eyes and glanced at his surroundings. There was a break in the gray skies and in the storm though strong winds still created whitecaps on the rough waters. This wasn't going to be a Sunday afternoon ride, but with God's help, he could do this.

The boat started up again and before Jake could comprehend that this was really happening, Flanagan shoved him over the side.

Overboard.

He gauged the drop and at the right moment, pulled in a long breath, filling his lungs. He slammed through the surface of the cold water, the shock of it jolting through his body. Then pain sliced through his arm sockets as *The Buccaneer* took off, dragging Jake along with it. He searched through the murky darkness, hoping to see something—ocean garbage or a sunken boat—anything at all that he could use to cut himself free. But then he'd risk getting entangled.

It was no use. The bottom of the sea was too deep and dark for him to see anything.

Squeezing his eyes shut, he did the only thing he could

do. Pray. He recalled scriptures from Isaiah he'd memorized years ago.

When you pass through the waters, I will be with you…

If he died now, if this didn't turn out like he hoped, there wasn't anyone to stand between Kelsey and those men.

No, Jake wouldn't think like that. He had to survive.

Lungs burning, the oxygen he held was quickly depleting. They screamed now.

His body grew numb as cold water rushed by him. *The Buccaneer* continued on like they'd forgotten him. Had they intended to leave him in the water from the beginning?

The tug on his wrists lessened until it finally stopped. Idiots! He had a good set of lungs on him and knew how to hold his breath. Anyone else would be dead by now.

He forced himself up to the surface and on his back to float in the ocean, and gasped for breath, fighting the waves. Darkness edged the corner his vision.

Somewhere in the distance, Kelsey screamed his name.

EIGHT

Strong arms gripped Kelsey, holding her back from getting to Jake as Flanagan and Ritter dragged him up and onto the boat. They dropped him onto the deck like he was nothing more than a big fish.

He didn't move, appearing lifeless. *Oh, God, please no!* Then, he started coughing up water, and Kelsey whimpered with both anguish and relief.

She'd threatened Lennon that if they didn't pull him up she would never cooperate. She couldn't be sure if he'd had his men stop the boat and fish Jake from the water because of her, or if he realized he'd probably already pushed Jake to the limit. How had he survived so long?

Dripping wet and shivering, Jake rolled onto his back.

"Let me go!" she screamed.

Lennon obliged, letting Kelsey free, and she ran to Jake, dropping to his side. She hugged him, not caring that he was icy cold and soaking. She peered up at Lennon, hating that she was so dependent on his mercy, if you could even call it that. "We have to get him inside, get him warm."

The way he looked at her, Kelsey almost wanted to take back her request, but she couldn't. Jake needed this.

"She's right, boys. We don't want him to end up like Neely."

Kelsey turned her head aside, hating to think about what they'd done to Captain Neely. "And what about his wife?"

She'd been afraid to ask about the woman, but she had to know.

"She's long gone. Got away. That's why we came for you, love."

"Please, stop calling me that." *I'm not your "love."*

He grinned, that loathsome, maniacal grin. Flanagan hefted Jake to his feet and practically dragged him away. Kelsey made to follow, but Lennon held his arm out, stopping her. What was his real name, anyway?

"I did something for you," he said. "Now tell me what you know. I can't promise the outcome won't be dire for your friend next time."

He'd done something for her? Acid burning inside, Kelsey stared at the wet deck, soaked with seawater Jake had left behind from his battle with the waters. She looked out over those waters and saw that they were where the Salish Sea met the Pacific, in the Strait of Juan de Fuca—the channel connecting the sea with the ocean. The channel separating Canada and the United States. Finally, she met the man's gaze. "Do you think I would have kept what I knew from you all this time?"

He studied her long and hard. "No. But I have a feeling you're going to start remembering something soon."

She pursed her lips. "Can I go now? I can't think when I'm worried about him."

"I don't really want to hurt anyone. I just want the map. Neely wasn't supposed to die, but since he did, I'm in all the way now, nothing more to lose. You understand what I'm saying?"

Why was he explaining himself to her? As if his reasons would change her opinion of him. Kelsey said nothing, but instead headed below deck. Lennon let her go. In the corner of her eyes, she saw him move to the helm. Where was he taking the yacht? Or were they just out on the water for privacy while they tortured her and Jake for information about the stupid map?

Descending the steps into the galley, Kelsey could hear the big burly henchmen guffawing about their fun with Jake. Had they hurt him again?

"Stop it!" she yelled, and glared at them. "You had your instructions, didn't you? Put him on the bed."

She wasn't sure where the boldness came from. Maybe she'd had enough of their treatment, or maybe she was a little emboldened with the fact that Lennon had responded to her pleas. Her requests. Kind of creepy, but there it was.

Jake climbed to his knees and stood on his own. From his hunched posture, she had a feeling they'd taken an opportunity to kick him while he was down. She ignored their leers and followed Jake into the small room where he collapsed on the bed, again, and this time soaking it with seawater. She grabbed blankets from the storage drawer under the bed, but hesitated before throwing them on Jake.

"Jake," she whispered. "You need to get out of the wet clothes. I'll see if I can get my hands on something belonging to Captain Neely."

His eyes were closed. He had to be exhausted, and considering his lips were blue, he was chilled to the bone. She pressed her hand against his shoulder and his lids flew open.

"I'm going to see about getting you something warm to drink," she said softly, "and the dry clothes, okay?"

She turned to walk away but his hand flew out and he grabbed her wrist. "No. Stay here. I don't want you near those men without me."

She didn't have the heart to tell him that whether he was there or not, he couldn't stop the men.

Even in his current state, he tossed her a cute, dimpled grin. Her heart flipped. "I've got a plan now," he said.

"A plan? When did you come up with that?" While he was in the water, being dragged behind the boat?

She slipped her hand into his, hating that he was still a little cold, but he was quickly warming up, which was good—he obviously had a good metabolism, and was in great physical condition. "Now tell me your plan, but keep it down. Ritter's still out there, I think, and Lennon, too."

"They'll need to refuel soon, won't they?" He spoke so softly, she had to lean close. "Whatever the reason, they're going to stop somewhere. Their guard will be down if they think I'm incapacitated."

Kelsey eyed him as he rested, flung out on the bed, looking for all the world like he'd come close to drowning, and she didn't even want to think about the beating he'd received. "Are you telling me you're not?"

He closed his eyes as though unconscious, leaving Kelsey to wonder if he was acting, or if he'd really blacked out. After everything he'd been through, she wouldn't be surprised he had. Regardless, he needed to rest and she'd leave him to it.

Kelsey went to the door and stepped through. It seemed kind of strange to have the freedom, and she wondered if she'd be punished. Lennon stood against the kitchen counter, holding a cell to his ear. How could she get her hands on that phone to call for help? And who was he communicating with?

Crossing his arms, he ended the call then turned his attention to her. "What now?"

He hadn't called her "love." She wasn't sure if that was a good or bad sign.

"I need access to the kitchen, and some of Captain Neely's clothes," she said, keeping her voice steady and measured. "I want to make Jake something warm to drink, heading off the risk of hypothermia. He needs something dry to wear, too."

He motioned for her to step from the room, and she walked by him as he closed the door behind her. That scared her—they'd kept the door open this whole time. Maybe this wasn't a good idea. She moved toward Captain Neely's quarters but paused, looking back at Lennon. He motioned for her to go ahead.

Kelsey stepped through the door to the master suite. She could tell the men had used it for their sleeping quarters. Mrs. Neely always kept the bed made, and the sheets were rumpled and the room just smelled—someone needed a shower. For the first time she considered that it was a small kindness they'd been left in the forward stateroom to themselves. Aware that Lennon watched her, Kelsey tore her gaze from the unkempt bed and moved to the closet.

When she opened the door, she gasped. It looked like it had been hit by a tornado. Most of the clothes had been piled on the floor.

"Nobody felt it was worth the effort to hang them up after we pulled everything from the closet to look for his hidden safe."

Had her clothes been dumped on the floor in her closet, too? She hadn't even looked.

Kelsey didn't want to talk about the map or its where-abouts; she wanted to focus on Jake. She knelt on the floor and searched through the pile for slacks, a belt and a shirt for Jake. Captain Neely and Jake were roughly the same size. Kelsey stood again and shook the clothes out. A white button-down shirt with blue stripes and jeans should look good on Jake—she almost rolled her eyes that she'd even considered how he would look in these. What did that matter?

Her eye caught a few nautical items—a lighthouse statue and a brass compass—on the floor by the bed. "Your men left those but threw the clothes back in the closet?"

"That worthless junk must have fallen off the shelf during the storm." He took his glasses off and smiled at her, then took a step toward her.

Kelsey rushed past him, praying with everything in her that he wouldn't try to stop her. She had to get out of this room with him.

In the galley, Kelsey hurried toward the stateroom where

Jake waited. "I'm leaving the clothes for Jake, and I'll be back to make the drink."

"Go ahead and make me something too while you're at it. This will give us a chance to talk in private."

Jake still appeared to be sleeping. She left the clothes in the cabin and returned to the galley, leaving the door open just a little. Lennon sat on the sofa waiting. Feeling his watching eyes, she tried to ignore the prickles along the back of her neck. She wanted him to have compassion for her. For them. But garnering his interest could be more than dangerous. She leaned against the kitchen counter and shut her eyes, blocking out the terrifying images of what could lie ahead for her and Jake.

Steadying her trembling hand, she reached into the cabinet to pull out packets of powdered hot chocolate. After microwaving two cups of water she added the hot chocolate and grabbed the two mugs. She turned and took a step back to the room where Jake was waiting.

"Where do you think you're going?" the man asked.

"To give Jake the drink, like I said." Though she'd hoped to avoid the private talk he wanted, she made her way the few steps to the table and handed him the other cup of hot chocolate.

"He can wait," he said. "You can drink his while we talk."

She wasn't sure that Jake could wait, but arguing would only waste time. If sitting with this man would get her back to Jake more quickly, then she'd oblige. Swallowing the lump in her throat, she slid in behind the dining table and across from him, warming her hands against the mug that had been meant for Jake.

Kelsey stared into the cup, aware of this dangerous man's intense scrutiny. When would this end? Unfortunately she knew the answer to that—it would end when she provided him with the information he wanted to know. Information she didn't have.

What would he do to her if she didn't think of anything to help him find the map? And where were they going? They had to be taking her and Jake somewhere—to meet someone, perhaps? "Where are you taking us?"

"If I get the map, I won't make you go the rest of the way." He adjusted his glasses, and thank goodness, he didn't grin.

She wouldn't go the rest of the way? What did that mean? Was he planning to throw her and Jake overboard? Closing her eyes, Kelsey sipped the hot chocolate slowly, wanting to leave some for Jake. She could reheat the drink. Again her mind was like a blank canvas. Any clues to the map were erased by the terror she and Jake had to endure.

"I don't think I know anything that will help you." What must the map be worth for this man to risk going to prison? Or to kill for?

"What do you know about Burroughs?"

"I don't think he's involved in Captain Neely's smuggling, if that's what you're asking." Kelsey imagined how Davis would react once he found out what Neely had been using *The Buccaneer* for.

"Then you're more naive than I thought."

"Naive? So that means you don't think I'm involved, after all?"

He didn't answer her but studied her behind his round glasses. "Your articles on your computer. I read them. They're very good."

What did she say to that, "Thank you?" She really didn't feel like having a pleasant conversation with the guy. Kelsey sipped more hot chocolate, hating that she was downing Jake's drink, but this man made her uncomfortable enough to need the distraction the drink offered.

"Every article and the accompanying photographs take place at a connection point," he said.

Kelsey tensed. "A connection point?"

"A point of contact for the smuggling operation."

Dread engulfed her. She was the one drowning now—she couldn't breathe. "No, no, that can't be."

Kelsey covered her face with her hands. He'd already told her the passengers were handpicked. A pang of hurt and anger twisted her throat. She couldn't speak the name on her lips.

No, Davis…

When she opened her eyes, Lennon looked on like he'd caught her red-handed, exposed her.

She gave a slight shake of her head. "I didn't know. I swear, I didn't know. That was the assignment Davis gave me." She begged for the hundredth time, pleading with this man who acted insane with the way he enjoyed seeing Jake suffer one minute, and then switched into a professional, a businessman she might meet on the street.

Jake was depending on her right now, and for him, she would tell this man what he needed to know so she could somehow buy them time to escape and survive. She drew in a breath, forcing out the trauma of the past few hours.

"Please, I'll help you, if I can, but it's clear I was used as a pawn here, and nothing more."

"How did you meet Burroughs?" he asked.

"I…I don't understand how that matters. How—"

"Just answer the question!" Veins in his neck bulged.

Kelsey froze, swallowed.

That was the first time he'd raised his voice to her. He tugged his glasses off and squeezed the bridge of his nose. Clearly, he was under serious pressure from someone to deliver this item. He'd kept his patience with her so far, but Kelsey didn't want to push him if she didn't have to.

"It's like when people choose a password, they often pick from the familiar. A pet's or a child's name, or some combination. There are clues in their lives that hold the key. In that way, they often telegraph their secrets."

"Telegraph?" Kelsey struggled to follow him.

"Indirectly communicate things. I need something that

will help me track the map. You see, I'm not so sure Neely had made his connection yet to that particular item."

"You mean you're not even sure it's on the boat? Then why are you keeping us?"

"Burroughs's yacht holds the key to finding the map—here or elsewhere—and so do you, somewhere in your pretty little head."

She wanted to ask him what *he* knew about Davis. Turn the questions around on him. That might actually do more to help them discover something. But she feared his reaction. She closed her eyes, and shoved away the dread curdling in her soul.

For Jake. Remember something…for Jake.

An image flashed in her mind—she and Davis at the museum the first time they met. He was admiring a famous Swiss artist. *Angelica Dietrich.*

Kelsey's eyes snapped open and stared into Lennon's dark ones minus the glasses. He was cleaning them now, with the corner of his shirt.

"The first time I met Davis…" Kelsey's words caught in her throat.

The print on the wall—by Dietrich. It hung directly across from her. Probably bolted in place to endure inclement weather. She didn't want to *telegraph* her thoughts by glancing at it—but maybe the print had clues. She allowed her gaze to drift around the room. No way would the map be hidden inside or behind the print—that would be too obvious. Wouldn't it? They had to have checked that already, and they'd come to the conclusion that Captain Neely had stashed it somewhere else. But what if they were wrong and missed something?

Could it still be on the boat? Could it be that easy?

No. The men would have discovered it.

"Yes?" He leaned forward, becoming impatient again, and

Kelsey knew she needed to give him an answer. Maybe not *the* answer, but *an* answer.

"The first time I met Davis was in a coffee shop. I spilled coffee on his shirt when I stumbled over his briefcase. So you see, he didn't pursue me and assign me to *The Buccaneer* for any other reason than to write my articles."

Doubt slid into his gaze and he leaned back, appearing to contemplate her words.

As she stared at what had to be tethered anger in his expression, she wanted to tell him what really happened, how they really met. There had to be an answer there. This guy knew more about Davis, her boss, than she did. But she couldn't give him the information. Not yet. The answer might have something to do with the artist and the print. It was a long shot at best, but it was all she had.

She would only play that card at the end, if she had to. If they couldn't escape.

"You're lying," he said, simply.

That's all it took to strike terror in her heart. Kelsey had never been so terrified in her life—this man was the only thing standing between her and his brutal goons. The only reason she and Jake were still alive. Was it worth the risk? Holding on to this one sliver of information?

"No." Her voice shook. "I'm telling the truth!"

He grabbed her forearm and squeezed. "If you're telling me the truth and you have no information to trade for your life then that news isn't going to go over well with…"

He didn't finish. Who? Go over well with who? She had a feeling it was someone even more powerful and dangerous.

"I don't understand." Her quickening pulse threaded around her throat. "Aren't you in charge? Can't you let us go?"

He squeezed harder. Angry with her, or angry with the situation, she didn't know.

"You're hurting me." She feared it was nothing compared to what he had in store for her.

* * *

You're hurting me...

Jake stood behind the door and listened, ready to come to her defense. Hesitating, he squeezed the knob, his palm slicking against the brass. If he barged in there now, he might blow the one chance they had.

He eased his hand away, knowing that he'd be by Kelsey's side in an instant if she *really* needed him.

Let go of her, come on, come on, come on...

Jake ticked off the seconds, his decision to wait gnawing at him. Then...finally...the man must have released Kelsey's arm. And Jake released a breath.

Some hero he was turning out to be. But in his own defense, he'd been caught off guard at first, beaten down before he'd been given a chance to be a hero. He was more prepared now. It was time to turn things around. But he couldn't do that if he revealed his quick recovery now.

He hoped Kelsey would agree to his plan to fool their abductors into thinking Jake wasn't worth their attention. Once they let down their guard, Kelsey might have a chance to get away. Jake, too, he hoped, but giving her a chance was all he cared about right now.

Watching Kelsey and the man she'd named Lennon through the crack in the door, the way he looked at her, the way he responded to her pleas, realization dawned.

Jake tensed. The man who abducted them was beginning to care about Kelsey. Acid boiled up. She'd better not be planning to use that to her advantage—it could work against her in a million ways.

Kelsey slipped from the seat and headed toward the door. Jake made his way back to the bed, slid under the covers. He'd already changed into Captain Neely's clothes—they were a little big, and it was a little weird wearing them. But they were dry.

He shut his lids enough to look like he was asleep, but he could still see what was happening.

The door swung open all the way, and Kelsey paused in the doorway. "Give me some time. I'll figure this out."

"We're almost there, and I need answers. Time is something you don't have, love."

NINE

"Where?" she asked. "Almost where? I can't help you—"

He shoved her all the way in the room but instead of shutting the door, he left it partially open like they wanted to hear her conversations with Jake, but still give them the illusion of privacy. Crazy. Or maybe Lennon himself wanted the privacy, but wanted to watch them, too.

Kelsey glanced down at the cup in her hands. She'd not gotten the chance to reheat it—still, it was warm enough to do Jake some good. She moved to the bed where Jake remained nestled under covers, sleeping. She lightly touched his shoulder.

"Jake," she whispered. "I brought you something warm to drink."

He didn't move. She wasn't sure if she should let him sleep or wake him. Kelsey set the mug on the built-in table next to the bed and sat on the edge. Leaning over, she pressed her face into her hands.

Lord, help us get out of this. I don't know what to do. Show us the way.

No answering peace dropped into her thoughts or soothed her heart.

She sat back up and watched Jake. Kelsey reached for his hand and held it, feeling the strength there despite his lack of response. He'd come so close to drowning, she couldn't stand to think about it.

But she let that reality sink in and with it, the memories of their time together. "I'm sorry things didn't work out for us," she said, softly. "I loved you so much, I thought I would die when things ended between us. But I survived."

Only to see the day come where they both would die together if they didn't escape.

Jake's hand tightened around hers and squeezed. *He's awake?*

He opened his amazing blue eyes and grinned.

He heard me. "You were pretending to sleep? To be unconscious?" The lout. She tried to move away but he tightened his grip.

"Isn't that what we agreed I should do?" He kept his voice low and glanced at the door. "So when the time is right, their guard will be down and I can take them by surprise. We can escape. Remember?"

"Yes. No. I don't know. I never agreed to that."

Kelsey tugged, attempting to ease her hand from his solid grip, hoping that would free her from the momentary power he held over her, but he wouldn't let go. She hadn't meant for him to hear the words, though he might already know the truth. She was still raw from almost losing him once more.

Only this time it would have been permanent.

Forever.

She couldn't bear the thought of his death.

His gentle gaze caressed her face and settled on her eyes. She wanted to turn away, but his searching look kept her captive. "I'm sorry things didn't work out, too. If something happens to me…" he said, letting his words trail off.

"Don't even say that." This time she succeeded in easing her hand from his.

"Kelsey, listen to what I have to say," Jake had spoken too loudly, and grimaced, glancing at the half-opened door. Then softer, "If something happens to me, I want you to know that you meant everything to me. I wanted to tell you before, but I was afraid the time wasn't right. But if anything happens, I might not…get another chance and you need to know…you were always the only one. Are…"

Are the only one? Why didn't he finish? No, she didn't want him to finish what he was going to say, did she? "You weren't supposed to hear what I said. I thought you were asleep."

"I have to be convincing. We need this to work." His words barely above a whisper, he shot her that grin that always made her knees weak and shaky.

Her insides trembled. She couldn't believe he still affected her this way. Did he suspect? Or did he *know?*

"But I'm glad you survived," he said.

Even when—and she would think *when* instead of *if*—they were free from this ordeal, she wasn't sure if her heart would survive.

He sighed. "I'm glad you moved on and made your dreams come true."

While she believed his words, she saw something else in his expression. Something she didn't want to see. Not really. He believed she'd moved on and had let go of her feelings for him, and left him behind completely. He really was glad for her, despite the hurt that played across his features.

Tears burned her eyes, but she held them back, not wanting Jake to see how he affected her.

Time to change the subject.

"I think I might know where the map is."

His expression hardened. "That's not what you told Lennon. And, yes, I was listening at the door."

"So you know I didn't tell him much."

"I know that he's on to the fact that you lied. Which means we're out of time. Why didn't you tell him?"

* * *

Jake grabbed the cup holding the tepid chocolate drink and sipped while he waited for her answer.

"Then they wouldn't need us anymore. That's all we—"

Jake held up his palm. "I agree with you, just wanted to hear it from you. You are planning on telling *me,* aren't you?"

A noise outside the door drew his and Kelsey's gaze over. Kelsey sat next to him in silent agreement that they should keep their voices down. But it was hard to concentrate on their plans when she was so close to him. Clearly their emotions were battered from many fronts—not the least of which was the feeling he still harbored for this woman.

He desperately wanted to know where she stood—if she still loved him as she once had. Jake steeled himself against the onslaught of tumultuous thoughts. He had to focus. Why did he have to battle this crazy desire right now with their lives in lethal danger?

Kelsey leaned forward and whispered, "You were right about Davis. He's involved, after all."

"You think?"

Her eyes flashed at his sarcasm.

He understood why she'd so easily and readily trusted her boss when she'd so quickly distrusted Jake. But that didn't mean he liked it.

"I don't know what I think anymore. Maybe I've got it all wrong."

"Never mind who's to blame. Just tell me what you know."

"I wasn't lying when I said I met Davis at a café when I spilled coffee on him. I just left out that afterward, we ended up at the museum next door, and then met there on occasion, and became friends. He admired a Swiss artist—one of his favorites. There's a print of her work in the galley." Kelsey tilted her head toward the door.

Jake shook his head. "So?"

"Don't you see? There could be a connection."

"There could be no connection. He likes the art, so he has it on *The Buccaneer*."

Kelsey harrumphed. "What is it with men?"

She rose from the bed and paced the small room, rubbing her neck.

"Okay. Let's go with it. What if it's true and the print is connected." He'd just humor her a bit if it meant discovering what they needed to know.

Kelsey dropped her hand. "Don't you see? That's just it. They think they got Neely before he got the map. They're convinced it's not even on board. They want to know where it is."

"They would have looked at the picture, too. I would have looked if given the chance. And in that case these jokers would have already found the map. That just seems too obvious to me."

"Obvious how?"

"A map hidden behind the picture? Come on, every B mystery movie made has something hidden in the artwork."

"That's not what I mean. I'm talking about the print giving something away about Davis. And that gives me—someone who knows him—an idea of where he might hide the items he smuggles. That is, if the map isn't the only thing."

"Why would anyone give away a clue like that?"

"I don't know. Maybe they do it without realizing it. Do you want to know what I think, or not?" Kelsey started coughing. "Do you smell smoke?"

Jake jumped up, no longer caring about his ruse. He smelled it, too. "Could be the engine, or could be electrical."

He thought he heard a distinct choppiness in the engine noise. Either way, he didn't want to be left to die on a burning boat. Kelsey's eyes grew wide with realization. She moved to the door.

He grabbed and pulled her back. "Kelsey, this could be it. This could be our chance. We have to play this right. Hold on…"

Jake glanced through the porthole. "We're heading toward land."

"Could be this is where they were heading to begin with. So our time is up anyway," she said.

"I see a rickety abandoned dock—can't imagine this would be anyone's destination. This is more like an emergency stop."

Fear creased across her pale face and instilled him with enough adrenaline for a real escape this time. He knew this was it.

"We're really going to do this, aren't we?" she asked, her eyes begging him for the answer.

"Yes. We're getting off this boat."

"What should we do first?"

"They're going to be preoccupied with the engine trouble and bringing the boat in to the dock, if they even know how to handle a rig this size."

Jake considered his options. He and Kelsey could bide their time and escape under cover of darkness. Maybe. Or make a break for it now.

The next few minutes, seconds even, could seal their fate. This was too big for him to decide without more guidance from above. He was man enough to admit he couldn't do this on his own.

He took Kelsey's hands in his. "Let's pray."

A slight curve lifted her lips. "That's the best idea you've had so far," she said.

Jake closed his eyes, embracing the warmth her words had given him. And…he prayed.

Prayed for guidance and direction.

For their safety.

And silently, he prayed that no matter what, Kelsey would escape unharmed.

When he raised his lids and looked into her glistening eyes, she smiled softly and stepped closer, wrapping her arms around him. She pressed her face against his chest, and Jake completed the embrace, holding her to him, wishing he never had to let her go.

But he would have to, when this was over.

One way or another.

TEN

Kelsey held tighter and breathed in the scent of this man she once...*still?*...loved. But how could they ever erase their past?

The lights in the cabin blinked on and off. Kelsey's pulse ramped up.

"I'm scared, Jake." The words slipped out. Of course she was scared—this had been a nightmare. But smoke or possible fire added fuel to the fear factor.

"We're getting out of this, just keep praying."

"We need to find out what's going on. I don't want to die from smoke inhalation while we wait."

"We're not waiting." Jake released her and gripped her arms. "This is it. Remember what we talked about? Me appearing too injured to be a threat?"

"So you really want to do it like this?"

"Have you got something better? Because so far my face-things-head-on efforts haven't done any good."

"You haven't exactly had a fair fight. So let's even the odds. Getting hold of a gun would help." *Or the electro-shock weapon.*

"I like the way you think." Jake grinned, though apprehension flickered behind his eyes.

This had to work.

But instead of climbing into the bed again, he quietly shut the door then searched the storage compartments underneath and then the closet. No one interrupted them. Like he said, they were too distracted at the moment to pay attention.

"What are you doing?"

"Looking for anything useful we'll need to take with us. Survival stuff." A noise resounded from the galley.

He scrambled under the covers again, and Kelsey stood at the door, her hand on the knob. She eyed Jake who stared back at her. Was he as uncertain about this as she was? How did he think he would gain the upper hand in that position? Was she supposed to lure someone over to the bed?

Kelsey coughed again. Facing Lennon and the two big jerks with him didn't seem nearly as threatening at the moment compared to the thought of burning on this boat.

Before Kelsey opened the door, it swung wide inward, knocking her back. Flanagan's bulky form filled the doorjamb while the muzzle of his gun filled her vision. She swallowed.

"What's going on in here? Keep the door like this so we can watch you," he said. "If you know what's good for—"

Kelsey flew into a racking fit of coughing. "There's smoke in the cabin." She choked out the words.

He glanced behind Kelsey to look at the bed where Jake pretended to sleep.

"We need some fresh air. Let us above deck."

"That's not possible." He shoved Kelsey out of his path and edged into the room. "Is he still out of it?"

She moved toward Jake, hoping to entice Flanagan all the way over. That was what Jake wanted, wasn't it? She peered at his seemingly unconscious form.

"He needs medical attention." Kelsey almost winced at her words—why would this man care?

"He's worthless." Flanagan inched closer. "Maybe I should just drop him overboard for good."

Their plan was backfiring. Kelsey needed to draw Flanagan's attention away from Jake. "Can you tell me what's going on? What's with the smoke? When are you going to let us go?"

Ignoring her, he nudged the blanket back with the muzzle of the gun. "Get up, you worthless—"

In one swift maneuver, Jake sprung forward and whipped the gun around on Flanagan, snapping it from his grasp.

Kelsey stifled a scream, knowing that she couldn't signal the others. Was this really happening? Had they finally gained some ground?

She watched the galley through the still-open door, praying the others wouldn't investigate. But it was like Jake had said—they were preoccupied with other matters. Jake pressed the gun into the bigger man's temple and forced him against the wall.

Would Flanagan make noise? Call for help, essentially calling Jake's bluff? At least she thought Jake was bluffing—she didn't think he would really kill the guy.

He fingered the trigger guard.

Prickles of dread surged up her spine. "You can't."

Would her words stay his hand? She moved in to make her point, but he pushed her back with his free arm.

She wanted to believe they would come out of this without harming anyone. Or was that just wishful thinking? Flanagan's hateful glare skewered Jake.

"You're not going to shoot me." Flanagan ground out the words, but sweat trickled down his temple.

"Jake, no. You can't shoot him."

"You're right," he said.

Jake slammed the butt of the weapon against the guy's head. Flanagan slid to the floor. Kelsey covered her mouth, muffling her outburst.

Jake gave her a stony look. "He'll live, and this way we don't have to worry about him alerting the others."

Seeing Jake with a gun gave her chills—but this was all necessary, she knew. He did this for them. For her.

His expression softened. "Let's get out of here."

"But how are we going to get by the other two?"

"We'll figure that out as we go. We've been given a chance to put our lives back into our own hands and we're taking it." Jake's gaze searched behind her. "Grab that first aid kit."

"First aid kit?"

"Hurry," he said and moved to the door, gun raised and ready. "We could be stuck in the wilderness for days. What we really need are the ten essentials. A map, compass, flashlight, knife…" Jake's voice trailed off. "We don't have time to gather all that. Just grab the kit. We need to make a quick escape."

"The wilderness?"

"Yeah. We must be somewhere along the Olympic Peninsula in Washington. Olympic Wilderness is well, a wilderness area, but it's also a national park. The good news is that tens of thousands of people visit the area every year so maybe we can find help."

"And the bad news?"

"It covers almost a million acres. We could run into trouble before we run into anyone, especially since the summer months are over. But first, we have to get away from these maniacs."

He sounded like a geography wiz. Kelsey searched through the bathroom cabinets until she found where she'd stashed the small kit. They were in survival mode, after all, and Jake had at least thought this part through.

Her chest tightened—they still hadn't figured out where the map was, but did that matter now if they were getting away from these men? Jake waited at the door as Kelsey grabbed her jacket from the small closet. She stuffed the soft case of the small first aid kit inside. Did they have time to stash some food in their pockets, too?

Stretching his arm toward her, he motioned for her to come on. She nodded and closed the distance. Holding the weapon like a pro in his right hand and Kelsey's hand in his left, he crept through the galley. She looked at the table and spotted the deck of cards but not Captain Neely's weapon. No cell phone, either.

The Swiss artist's print on the wall snagged her thoughts—an unintentional clue? She thought about Lennon's earlier words. The painting Davis had admired at the museum had been of a lighthouse.

"Wait," she said, pulling free from Jake's hand.

She paused to stare at the print. "I know where it is."

"Leave it." He snatched her hand back.

Kelsey tugged free again and hurried to Captain Neely's quarters. She lifted a jacket from the closet and tossed it to Jake.

"What are you doing?" he whispered as he tugged on the jacket. "We don't have time for this."

She bent to pick up the lighthouse statue forgotten on the floor. Lennon had called it worthless junk.

"This isn't worth our lives," Jake whispered. "Let them have it."

"It just might be the price for our survival, the price for us getting off this boat." Kelsey searched the cheap ceramic gift from a tourist shop, looking for a hidden compartment. She found the top twisted off, but when she looked inside…

Nothing.

"I don't understand," she said.

"Let me have that." Jake grabbed the lighthouse.

Any second wasted increased the chances he might have to use more than the butt of a gun. He didn't want to shoot anyone and he definitely didn't want to risk placing Kelsey in harm's way, so the sooner they got away, the better.

Through the window he noticed the sky had grown dark, and droplets of rain gathered against the glass. They were running out of what little time they had to pull this off. He pressed the statue against the edge of the built-in headboard until it cracked, hoping they could find whatever it was she was looking for and leave.

A small canister fell from the crumbling plaster within the thickest part of statue—hidden in the obvious. The item in question? They weren't going to wait to find out.

He handed her the tube. "We have to leave. Now."

Someone ran down the steps.

Brilliant. Flanagan had finally been missed.

Jake pressed his back against the limited wall space behind the door, Kelsey barely squeezing next to him. Just to be clear, he held his finger to his lips. Through the crack between the door and the jamb, Jake spotted Ritter—the guy who wore the eye patch—in the bedroom across the way. No doubt he'd found his buddy unconscious on the floor.

Red-faced and growling, Ritter bolted from the bedroom and searched the galley as if Kelsey and Jake could have hidden there somewhere. Jake braced himself for the guy's next stop. Almost breathless with fury, Ritter rushed through the open door, and in that split second it took the man to register the room wasn't empty, Jake slammed the butt of the gun against his skull.

Jake caught a glimpse of Kelsey's disapproving expression. "What?" he asked. "You wanted me to shoot him instead?"

What did she expect? The guy would let them go with a simple request if they said please? Like he'd already told her, they had a chance and they were taking it.

Not wasting any more time, Jake eased into the galley and up the steps, prepared to face off with the last one—the man dubbed Lennon. The boat rocked as another storm stirred the water, but Jake suspected they'd docked against the shabby pier already. How Lennon planned to get any help with the engine trouble on this rig, he didn't know.

Didn't care.

As long as he and Kelsey found a way off *The Buccaneer* and away from these men, they'd be all right. He had to believe that. He hesitated before stepping above deck, Kelsey so close behind him he felt her warm, fast breath on his neck. Wanting to reassure her, he grabbed her hand and squeezed.

"Flanagan! Ritter! Get your lazy bums up here. I can't fix this by myself."

With the words, Jake knew where the man was and crept the rest of the way. While making a run for it right now with Kelsey seemed like a good idea—to jump off the boat and flee up the shaky pier like they'd done before—they couldn't escape without this man seeing them.

And shooting.

Lennon leaned over the engine hatch and cursed under his breath.

Jake lifted his weapon and took aim. He planned to hit Lennon over the head, like the others, but he had to be prepared to shoot if it came down to that. He risked a glance back at Kelsey to gesture for her to go. He'd catch up.

She shook her head.

Stubborn woman! She'd get them both killed.

When he glanced back, Lennon startled and whipped around, aiming his own weapon at Jake's head.

Standoff.

The grip grew slippery under Jake's moist palm. He should have acted when he'd had the chance. Now there was no way he could sneak up on the man.

"It's over," Jake said. "Your men are incapacitated below deck. I could have killed them, but I didn't. I don't want to kill you, either. Just let us go."

The man proffered that awful grin he always conjured when he looked at Kelsey. "Not until she gives me what I want."

At the innuendo, bile burned Jake's throat.

Kelsey stepped forward. "I found what you're looking for. You can have it if you throw your weapon overboard."

"Not gonna happen, love," Lennon said. Misty rain stuck to his glasses, making his eyes appear blurry behind them.

"If you don't want me to throw this into the ocean—lost to you forever—do as I say." Kelsey's forceful words surprised Jake.

"How do I know I can trust you?"

"I suppose that's a risk we both have to take," Jake said. "Kelsey, hand me the tube and then get off the boat. Start walking to the shore. I'll meet you there."

"Not without—"

"Do it!"

Tube in hand, he blinked rain and sweat from his eyes while he listened to her creaking footsteps on the pier. His finger grew slippery against the trigger guard. "We can both throw our weapons at the same time. Both have what we want. You can get the artifact and your money. We can walk off this boat alive. Agreed?"

Lennon's eyes shifted to something behind Jake. Had one of the men recovered? Or was he watching Kelsey leave? By his expression Jake *knew* he watched Kelsey.

Knew he wanted more than the canister from her. Blood roared in Jake's ears. He wanted to punch the smirk off the guy's face. But now wasn't the time to wipe her memory from Lennon's head.

"Whatever you say."

At the same time, Jake and Lennon spread their arms, lifting their weapons. Jake watched the man edge toward the side of the boat as did Jake.

"Now, drop it in the water." Heart rate soaring, Jake focused on the man in front of him. One mistake could end his life. Kelsey's life.

"You first." Lennon smirked.

"Together."

This wasn't the best way to go about it. There had to be a better approach, but he couldn't think of one. The others below deck wouldn't stay unconscious forever. In order to leave the boat, he'd have to toss the weapon, too. He didn't relish facing whatever was ahead without the protection, but he had no choice.

Five seconds, six, seven…ten seconds ticked by. It was now or never.

What if Jake released the gun and Lennon didn't? Would he have time to grab it back? Dive into the water?

Freedom was only a few steps away…if he didn't mess this up.

"I can see you don't trust me. Give me what I want and you can go. I'm going to drop my gun, too."

Jake held the canister over the water along with the gun. "If you don't let go and shoot me instead, the canister goes in the water, too. Understood?"

The guy adjusted his glasses. "Understood."

"Now." Jake released his weapon.

To his relief, Lennon also let go of his gun. Two splashes resounded as the weapons hit the water.

"Toss me the canister," Lennon said.

Jake took one step backward, keeping his focus on the man's gaze and movements. At this moment in time, he had the advantage. Another step, and then another step, and soon, Jake's next step would mean turning his back and running.

Oh, Lord, please let Kelsey be at a safe distance.

He hoped beyond hope for their freedom and survival. But a deep burning sensation swirled inside his gut, telling him this wasn't going to end well.

Now.

The time was now.

Jake tossed the canister in the air toward Lennon. The man lunged for it as Jake turned his back and sprinted across the deck.

He leaped from the boat.

Slammed into the dock.

Boards creaked beneath his feet. Behind him, Lennon yelled for Flanagan and Ritter. He wasn't going to let Jake and Kelsey go. But he'd have to catch them first. Jake had to get far enough away before the man got his hands on another weapon if that was his intention.

Jake pumped his arms and legs, sprinting for his life. The shore was too far. Jake would never make it.

I'm going to die.

He turned for a glimpse behind…

Gunfire resounded, magnified by a hard, jolting force, the pain blasting through his arm and across his chest.

ELEVEN

Sheets of rain pelted Kelsey's face. "Jake!"

Her shout erupted from a desperate place, but the crashing waves and storm drowned out her voice. Though they hadn't been enough to block the gunfire that had sliced through the air and still echoed in her ears. In that instant, Jake had turned sharply to the side, grabbed his left arm and staggered a few steps before he picked up speed and ran toward her.

When he reached her, he briefly caught her up in his arms then didn't miss another beat as he continued forward, dragging her along behind him. "Let's go."

The guy was invincible, it seemed, but Kelsey had to know. "Are you shot?"

Cold wind roared in her ears. Had he heard her question?

"Doesn't matter if we don't get away."

She heard the agony in his voice, even over the ocean waves that broke against the rocky shore. She didn't miss the anguish etched across his features. They hadn't gone fifty yards when he slowed, straggling next to her and glanced behind them. She followed his gaze. Resisting the waves, the boat remained moored to the rickety, forgotten pier.

No one was in pursuit.

She watched Jake's expression. He eased his gaze from *The Buccaneer* and scanned the length of the rocky driftwood-littered beach. Evergreens grew on top of a few large sea stacks, and the thick forest loomed ahead. Jake's frown confirmed what she dreaded. Why would the men bother pursuing them here—wounded, with no food and limited supplies, they were as good as dead anyway.

"Look. There's a small cave," she said. "We can get out of the weather and see to your wound."

Jake shook his head, his gaze drawn to his stumbling feet. "No, that cave will be underwater soon. The tide's coming up and the headlands will trap us here. We'll drown if we don't get off this beach."

The downpour slowed, giving them a reprieve, but they were already drenched. Kelsey looked around—she hadn't considered the tide.

"We need to disappear into the forest. Be well hidden in case they come after us. He still shot at me, even after he got the canister. I don't think he's going to just let us go." Jake scrutinized her, concern grazing his pained features.

Revulsion made her shiver at the thought of being trapped by Lennon again.

"Keep your voice down in case they follow." He stumbled forward and stepped into the thick, dripping canopy, stomping around huge ferns and dense undergrowth until he stood at the base of a tree. Moss grew everywhere, covering spruce and cedars alike.

Chilled to the bone in spite of her jacket, she rubbed her arms and was about to ask Jake if she could check his injury when he slipped his hand beneath the jacket and grimaced. Then he ran his hand over the back of his left arm. He'd been shot from behind, so…had the bullet gone all the way through his arm? Grazed his chest? What?

On shaky legs she took a step toward him. "We have to stop the bleeding."

He slumped against a tree. "Just bandage it up. We can't stay here too long."

Kelsey frowned. He wasn't going to listen, but they shouldn't go tromping through the woods until they'd tended his wound. She pulled the kit out and found some gauze and tape.

Jake shrugged out of the jacket and tugged his shirt off on the left side, exposing his arm and chest.

Kelsey swallowed and forced her attention to his gunshot wound. It had torn through his triceps, grazing his chest, too. "I should clean it first."

She reached for the kit and Jake grabbed her wrist. "No time. Just bandage it to slow the bleeding. Wrap the tape around tight, like a tourniquet."

Slow the bleeding, not stop the bleeding.

At least there weren't any major arteries or vessels there, but she was still unwilling to consider everything those words could mean. Kelsey focused on the task at hand and made quick work of taping the gauze against the wounds to his arm and chest. Then Jake pulled his bloody shirt back on, followed by the jacket. He stood. Swaying on his feet a little, he steadied himself against the tree and took off again, heading away from the shoreline.

The way he kept moving, it was hard to believe he'd been shot. Maybe adrenaline was pushing him to get them to safety, but an uneasy feeling clung to her.

Fallen moss-covered trunks littered the way, and Jake assisted her over the larger obstacles. Where the undergrowth and ferns were thick, leaves slashed against her face, slick and moist.

"Jake, wait. Stop." She slid to the cold, damp ground, trying to catch her breath. "I can't… We have to stop and rest." She wasn't the one who'd been shot. What was the matter with her?

His brooding gaze peered down at her—she *knew* he wanted to stop, too. He reached down and pulled her to her aching feet. "This is our chance to live, Kelsey. Do you want to end up back on that boat?"

How could Jake keep going like this? She admired his

strength and determination, though it put her to shame. From
her sore legs and back to the numb, cold tips of her fingers
and toes, she wanted to whimper instead of trek through the
wilderness. She grabbed the collar of the jacket he wore, and
he stumbled back. It seemed like he was trying to keep her
from getting too close.

He's hiding something.

"Jake," she said softly then tugged on the jacket. He didn't
resist this time as she lifted the heavy leather of the bomber
jacket that hid so well what she'd feared most. "You're still
bleeding. Jake…" The tremble in her voice magnified with
what she saw. Had she missed bandaging part of his wound?
"We have to stop the bleeding now."

He reached over and cupped her cheek, his face pale. Cold.
Yet his expression was warm. "It's just a flesh wound."

She pressed her hand over his, warming her cheeks. "You
don't have to save me, you know?"

A small laugh escaped him, accompanied by that grin that
always sent her heart racing. "And you don't need to worry
about me. I promise we'll stop to rest soon."

"I have a feeling you don't plan to stop until you finally
drop from exhaustion," she said. *Or something worse.*

He took her hand and rubbed it between his, warming it
up, then brought it to his lips. A lump formed in her throat.
Oh, Jake. Why had she ever let this man go? She knew she'd
had reasons—good ones—but she couldn't remember them
right now.

"Come on, let's get lost in this forest," he said.

He pushed forward like he lived to backpack in the wilderness. Maybe this was his sort of thing, but it certainly wasn't
her thing and she felt it to the marrow.

"Do you have any idea where we're going?" she asked.
"Did you really mean we should get lost in the forest?"

"This is one of the wildest places left in the country, aside
from Alaska. I always wanted to backpack here, that's why

I know. If you had your camera, this could make a great article."

"Maybe another time," she said. The pristine and lush temperate rain-forest environment took her breath away. Or maybe that was the fear…

"I want to make it to that high point." Jake pointed ahead of them. "So we could watch the boat from a safe distance, see if it's still there. See what they're doing. If they plan to follow. And we need to make shelter before actual nightfall. I don't think water's going to be a problem in the usual way."

Shaky and hoarse, his voice revealed his weariness and something bordering on defeat. That big strong Jake was about to break, unnerved her to the core.

Kelsey pressed her hand against another fallen log and grabbed something slimy. She jerked her hand back. "Ugh…"

"A banana slug. You squashed it. Don't you know you're not supposed to disturb the ecosystem?"

How could he be so playful? Grimacing, Kelsey swiped her hand against the moss. She'd have to watch what she was doing while battling exhaustion.

"How much farther? Do we really need to know if they're following us?"

"Yes."

"I don't think there's any question they will follow."

Ignoring her, Jake sluggishly hiked to the top of the ridge and stood amid the trees. Kelsey stepped up behind him, not willing to stand too close to the edge. The wind had died down and the rain had settled to a soft drizzle.

There didn't appear to be any life on the boat. Had the men already left? She glanced down at the shore—the tide had come in, cutting off the beach where they'd made their escape. Still, the north side of the shore remained accessible via the pier.

As they watched, one of the men stepped from below deck and hopped onto the shaky structure, followed by the other two. They headed for the beach. From this distance, she could tell that Lennon was the one leading them.

Jake shook his head. "Here they come. Even with the map, they still won't let us go."

Guilt washed over her like a storm-driven wave. She leaned against a tree, nausea swirling inside. Why had she taken the risk?

"Jake," she whispered, slipping her hand into his. "I made a terrible mistake."

He turned his head, pulling his gaze from their stalkers below. He looked like he was at the end of his rope. Either he didn't have much energy left, or he was seriously dreading what she had to tell him.

"What?"

She lifted her jacket, revealing an antique document, wrapped, preserved and sealed in plastic, and tucked in the inner pocket.

Jake's thoughts swirled in a vortex of confusion.

Focus, man. He squinted at the document—the map?—contained in a protective wrapping and protruding from Kelsey's inside pocket.

How had…when had…?

"Why didn't you tell me?" His eyes flashed up to see the bitter regret in hers.

Their big escape…trading the map for their lives…he'd taken a bullet…and it had all been a lie. No wonder Lennon was coming after them. He'd want the map *and* he'd want revenge for being tricked.

Her mouth opened, but nothing came out.

He stepped closer, reining in the harsh words he wanted to unleash. Grabbing her arms, he tugged her toward him so he could look her in the eyes. "How could you keep this from me? Why did you take it to begin with?"

"I'm sorry." The alarm in her eyes, on her face, sobered him.

"No. I'm the one who's sorry," he said, releasing his grip but not her pensive gaze. She was exhausted and frightened—yelling at her wouldn't change the past and it wouldn't do either of them any good.

And yet, there she stood holding on to the very thing the men were after. Jake ripped his gaze from her, unsure how to deal with the bombshell she'd just dropped.

He knew, too, that they probably should stop and see to his wound, but he was afraid to, until they'd gotten far enough away from the men. Until he'd gotten Kelsey to safety. Only then could he rest.

Maybe they'd come across hikers or a trail that would lead them to safety or a ranger station. He watched the waves crashing against the rocks.

Against *The Buccaneer*.

Maybe they could somehow make their way back down and take the boat themselves. No. That would be too risky. He couldn't know if the men had been able to repair the engine trouble. Then they'd be no better off than when they started.

"Jake." Kelsey said his name, but he couldn't look at her.

He weaved both hands through his hair to press against his still-pounding head, and felt the ache from his wound turning to a dull throb.

"Jake, there wasn't a chance for me to tell you. It happened so fast, and we've been running ever since. And after that, in the forest, I just wasn't thinking—"

He whirled on her now. "You're right. You weren't thinking."

"Maybe we can just leave it somewhere now. Leave it for them to find."

"That's not going to work." Jake stomped off down the hill. "They're hunting us now, and I'm already dead on my feet."

Kelsey stumbled behind him and he caught her, preventing her from tumbling downhill through the forest. He had to protect her.

He loved her. Okay. He admitted it now. He'd never stopped loving her.

That's why the ache of betrayal hit him anew with her revelation. Though she said she'd not intended to keep it from him, working against him like this, however inadvertently, served as a reminder of their past, of their trust issues.

"Jake, I thought…the map doesn't belong to smugglers. It belongs in the hands of the rightful owner, a museum somewhere. In that moment, when I had the chance to remove it from the canister, I thought I was doing the right thing. It was too late by the time I realized what a mistake I'd made."

He studied her beautiful hazel eyes, hating the grief he saw in them. Hating that he'd played even a small role in her distress with his reaction to the news. He'd give anything if he could simply forget the mistake that could cost them their lives, forget that men were after them, forget their past and sweep her up in his arms. But he couldn't just…forget.

And maybe this was how she'd felt when she'd seen Heather leaving his apartment. That wasn't something she could forget and go forward like nothing had happened.

She studied the mossy drenched earth. "It'll be dark soon, especially in the forest. Should we just find shelter like you said?"

"I'm not sure it's a good idea to stop, considering we're being hunted now."

"But they're not going to search for us in the dark. With the clouds, it'll be pitch-black out here. Isn't this where the Sasquatch lives?"

He almost smiled at her attempt to soften the edge. Soften his frustration with her. But he didn't respond. Didn't stop hiking.

At some point, Jake realized that Kelsey no longer followed. If he stopped moving, he wouldn't be able to get started again. But…she wasn't going to follow him. He couldn't continue walking without her and leave her behind, and she knew it.

Women.

Jake leaned over, propping his hands on his thighs, unsure how long he could continue. Kelsey was at his side in an instant. Or had it been much longer?

"Jake…" Her voice sounded distant. "There's a huge tree just up ahead. See it?"

He caught a glimpse of it then hung his head again. *Red cedar.*

"I've never seen one so big, but there's a crack or fissure that runs through it. Let's take cover in there."

Before, Jake had felt that he hadn't had any choice other than to keep moving. But now, he had to accept a measure of defeat.

At least for the moment.

With a base and trunk that rivaled any sequoia in the redwood forest, the cedar tree had to contain hundreds of cubic meters of wood, thick and twisted all the way to the crown. Jake watched as Kelsey carefully stepped over the gnarly root system that bulged out before plunging into the earth.

A branch hung low as though opposing their entrance into the tree cave and Jake held on to it for support. When he tilted his head just so, he could hear the sound of rushing water. "Wait," he said. "You wait here."

"Where are you going?"

Jake sighed, feeling too tired to explain. But he knew that if they were going to make it through, they would have to communicate better. To trust one another. So he'd give it a try.

"I'm going to gather some branches and ferns to cover up the opening and make it warm and comfy." Somehow he managed a small grin. The relief he saw in her eyes was reward enough.

"I can help you."

"No. Just sit here and rest. Conserve your energy. I'm

going to need you to be strong later." The look she gave him said she questioned his judgment. "I need you to trust me, Kelsey. Can you do that?"

The quiver began in his legs…

Strong. He had to be strong just a little longer. But he knew this drill. Had practiced it many times before.

Head, guts, heart.

Admittedly, he was entering that part of this ordeal that would require some guts.

She nodded her agreement, but not wholeheartedly.

"Good. Just hang loose here. I'll be right back."

"But where—"

Jake ignored her. Prayed she didn't follow. He *did* intend to find the branches and ferns, but they weren't the only reason he'd walked away. He also had to find that rushing water. Wash out this wound. He was risking infection either way. But he'd not wanted Kelsey to see it before he'd washed it off this time. Bad enough she'd seen it to begin with. Thank goodness this environment was cooler and not crawling with infectious organisms.

The roar grew as he drew near the creek until he spotted the stream swollen with rainwater. The trick would be how to get in and out without slipping or washing away with the flow. And it would be cold.

Very cold.

Jake stripped off the leather jacket belonging to the late Captain Neely and then his shirt, planning to wash it out separately. He didn't have a clue if he should remove the bandage or not, but figured the wound needed cleaning so he ripped the tape.

And gasped, dizziness sweeping over him.

Grabbing a protruding root, he tugged on it to make sure it would hold him and when he was sure, he plunged his upper body into the icy cold water—stifling the guttural moan that battled to escape lest Kelsey hear—and washed the blood from his torso and the wound.

A deep, bone-piercing throb crashed through him until he could no longer stand it and he tugged on the root, righting himself. He gasped for breath, grateful he hadn't passed out.

Next he plunged the shirt into the rushing water, scrubbing and rubbing it against the boulders near the bank to remove the caked-on blood. Satisfied it was clean enough, and shivering to the core, he tugged the jacket back on, leaving the shirt off for now, and trudged back to the cedar, hoping he hadn't just made a big mistake by washing his wound with water that wasn't sterile. One he could hardly afford.

But this was the cleanest water he could get his hands on, and he wasn't a doctor, so he didn't know what else to do. Back in the tree cave, Kelsey could clean it out with antiseptic wipes, layer it with antibiotics and bandage it. What more could he do until he got real medical attention?

Before he made sight of the tree, he removed the jacket to tug the shirt back on, his skin chafing against the cold material and welcoming it at the same time. Jake gathered sword fern branches and anything else useful he could find.

Kelsey stirred when she saw him—relief evident in her face, and yet, she was perturbed that she'd been made to wait on him. He knew her well enough to recognize that look. He spoke first to forestall her.

"Why don't you grab some moss and make us a soft place to rest inside the cave."

While she worked, he fashioned a lean-to against the opening, then covered even that with foliage to hide the tree cave in case Lennon and his men trekked this far into the forest. His task complete, Jake practically fell onto the moss bed Kelsey had arranged inside. She sat next to him, opening his coat up to see the damage the bullet had caused. Jake suspected it wasn't too bad or he couldn't have lasted this long. But what did he know?

"Oh, Jake," she said, her voice trembling. "What... How did you... What happened to the blood?"

He smiled, glad he'd washed it away. "I cleaned up while I was out. I need you to dress the wound with stuff from the first aid kit, okay?"

"Sure. Of course," came her soft reply, then the sound of her digging around in her jacket. "I can't really see in here that well, it's getting too dark."

"Just slather antibiotic on it and bandage it."

"Okay, but I need you to sit up and pull the jacket and your shirt off."

Jake exhaled and then, with her help, he shoved up and removed the jacket and shirt, exposing his wounds. He hoped he could sleep this weariness off, or else they were in big trouble.

Almost too tired and numb to feel the pain and her tenderness as she worked, Jake tried to be a good patient.

"There. I'm done," she said.

Words had never sounded so good. "Give me the kit."

She handed him the bag and he searched through until he found the small envelope containing a thermal blanket for treating hypothermia or shock, grateful the kit even contained one. With his last ounce of strength, he thrust his arm back into his jacket and crawled from the tree cave.

"Where are you going?"

"You sleep in the cave, I'll keep watch out here." Jake ignored her protests that she should guard them and shoved the lean-to back in place.

He found a large, gnarly moss-covered root and, after he shook out the blanket, he hunkered down against it. Inside the cave with her, he'd wanted to wrap her in his arms and kiss her. He needed to feel her tenderness. Leaving her so he could stand guard had been half an excuse.

A chill ran through him—something more than the cold. "I wish I could build a fire," he mumbled. He actually considered it for a minute.

But he just.

Couldn't.

Move.

Besides, a fire might bring the men to their cozy little tree cave. *Hold on. Just a little longer.* They were unprepared for the wilderness. In this season. With his bullet wound. Utterly unprepared.

Head, guts... He hoped it wasn't going to come down to *heart*.

TWELVE

Darkness overtook the rudimentary shelter—their only protection from the elements, and Jake had left it so he could be the one to stand guard. She'd wanted to protest, but she knew that tone he'd used, and arguing wouldn't get them anywhere. Exhaustion didn't bring sleep to her overworked mind, though.

Kelsey had made quick work of bandaging Jake's wound, and had tried to hide her distress at seeing the injury again. The man was too stubborn for his own good. They should have stopped to take better care of that immediately, but she understood his fear, and the risk. How much more he'd bled, she couldn't tell because he'd washed it all away before she could see. There were plenty of things she didn't have a clue about, but one thing she knew—blood loss and infection would be their main concern.

Don't forget the hijackers. Thieves. Looters. Murderers. Whatever they were called with their list of crimes.

And what should she call herself? Why had she taken that stupid map?

Her body ached along with her heart and mind. She blew out a breath. *Oh, Lord, please lead us out of this. Show us what to do.*

Oh, God, I can't lose him. The familiar surge of moisture threatened behind her eyes. She squeezed them tighter, but it was no use. Salty tears streamed down her cheeks. In this darkness, no one knew but her.

And God.

They were lost in what Jake said was the wildest place left in this country. And they weren't just up against the wilderness, dark, cold and rain. Men were hunting them.

Her stomach growled. But they had no food.

Could Jake hunt without tools, even if he had the skills? Did he know which berries were edible? She didn't. Why should she? Maybe someone who planned to hike in the national park or wilderness area would plan ahead for all possibilities, but getting lost in the wilderness was never in the realm of possibilities for Kelsey.

Nor was being pursued by killers.

The tears sliding across her face had grown into a river. Racking sobs threatened now, warring with her tired-to-the-bone exhaustion. Kelsey figured she had two choices. Give in to the sobs. Or succumb to fatigue.

For hours now, she'd fought both to be strong for Jake.

In case… In case he crumpled under the weight of his injuries. And that last thought, that last image, was the one to push her over the edge. The sobs won the battle line, finally pushing through.

Oh, God.…

She wanted to be strong, but maybe a girl was allowed a good cry now and then. Kelsey sighed, feeling the weight of the day closing in on her mind now like a big blanket. How could he be so strong? With a heavy heart, her mind drifted to sleep, barely hanging on to consciousness as she wrestled with one last thought.

What kind of woman was she to let a guy like him go—push him away, the way she had?

Gray light penetrated her thoughts.

She sat up on her elbows and scanned her surroundings.

She was still in the tree cave, her clothes damp. A rustling sound alerted her to Jake crawling into the lean-to. His lips formed into a full-on smile, but his haggard expression told her the smile was only meant to encourage her. Still, the man was as rugged and handsome as ever, even now.

"Feeling better?" he asked.

"I'm not the one who was beaten, dragged under water behind the boat and then shot."

His smile fell, and Kelsey instantly regretted her words. "Jake, I'm worried about you, that's all."

"Don't be. My health is the least of our worries." He opened his hand to reveal a few scrawny berries. "Hungry?"

"Are you sure they're okay to eat?" Though Kelsey was so hungry at the moment, she wasn't sure she cared.

"Don't you know a huckleberry when you see one? My grandmother lived in Oregon. We picked these along the coast when we'd visit her—and she'd make pies. Lots of pies." He scooted all the way into the cozy space and lay next to Kelsey, propping his head on his arm. "I used to love her huckleberry pies."

"I like blueberries." Kelsey popped a huckleberry into her mouth and savored the tart flavor. Unfortunately, it seemed to stir her hunger even more.

"Here, you take them." Jake tried to hand off the berries from his pockets.

"No. Let's share," Kelsey said. "I need you to be strong."

He eyed her, looking a little hurt. "Have I let you down yet?"

She looked at the berries. "No. You've been amazing." But how much longer could he keep up the act?

"Never question a guy's strength."

Glancing back up, she caught his grin. He was teasing, but she saw in his eyes the truth in his jest. She didn't want to argue with him. At least he joined her in finishing off the berries.

A small bit of huckleberry clung to his lip. Kelsey reached over and wiped it free. How strange that she was stuck in this crazy situation with Jake, of all people. How glad she was that it was him—not that she'd wish this on anyone, but Jake was the man she wanted by her side.

Kelsey swallowed, grappling with that realization for not the first time.

"What's the plan?" She hugged her knees to her chest.

"We keep going. All we have to do is find civilization or someone who can help, whichever comes first." He sat up, his face mere inches from hers. "I say we hug the coast as much as possible. While I hope we could stumble across a trail or hikers, I doubt that'll happen. If we can find the mouth of a river, there might be a town."

She drew in a breath. "The coast, huh?"

"Yeah, it's going to be rocky in places. You have to be in decent shape. I won't lie to you."

The way he stared at her... "You think I'm not in good shape?"

He grinned again. She loved that grin. "I think you take good care of yourself and have a great figure," he said.

Warmth spread over her, a warmth she both hated and appreciated. The guy always had known how to charm his way out of a sticky situation.

"But we both know what I'm talking about. Stamina. Reflexes."

"We're going to need both no matter which way we hike." Kelsey sighed.

He nodded. "Pretty much."

"What about your injury?" How was he going to keep going?

His expression grew somber. "Promise me if something happens—" his voice soft, he cleared his throat "—if I succumb to fatigue or this injury, you'll keep going and get to safety. Promise you'll be willing to leave me if you have to."

"No, Jake, no." She shook her head and crawled out of the tree cave. Pushing over the lean-to, she stood, free of the confined space. Free from Jake's penetrating gaze. "No…"

But he was right behind her. "I was afraid you were going to react like that, but I have to make sure we understand each other. You're going to survive this—"

"Jake?" She cut him off.

Brows knitting, he froze.

Behind him, a bear sniffed around the berry bushes not fifteen yards away.

THIRTEEN

Jake studied the bear.

About three hundred pounds. Black fur, but more importantly—no hump between the shoulders.

Black bear. Not grizzly.

He swallowed. That bought them a chance. One thing he knew, bears had an incredible sense of smell.

Had Jake's blood brought the animal near? No. That couldn't be it or Jake might be facing off with the beast right now instead of looking at him from a distance.

A short distance at that.

Making a lot of noise was the usual precaution to prevent running into bears or other potentially dangerous wildlife, letting the animal know you were coming. That usually scared them off well in advance. But apparently, they'd done too good of a job keeping their voices down because the bear hadn't reacted. Probably too preoccupied grabbing his last meal before hibernation.

Jake gripped Kelsey's hand and squeezed. Turning slowly to her, he lifted his finger to his lips. Backing away unnoticed while the bear was preoccupied was the best.

A twig snapped beneath. His foot or Kelsey's, he wasn't sure.

The bear pulled its head from the bushes. Not good.

The bear rose on its haunches looking fearsome. Jake's pulse notched up.

Hold it together. Kelsey's palm slicked against Jake's.

"Do *not* scream," he said, his voice low and even. "The bear's only trying to smell what kind of animals we are."

Jake took a slow step back. "And I'm talking right now to let it know we're humans. You are *not* interested in eating us today, are you, bear."

"But…but, I thought we're supposed to stand our ground and act big, scare them away."

"Do as I say. It depends on the situation and the kind of bear." Jake hoped he was right.

"We're backing away from you. Giving you a wide berth."

"We're backtracking?" Kelsey whispered, sounding incredulous. "But what about the men?"

He hadn't exactly said the word *backtracking,* but yeah, this was just that.

Another few steps and they would be hidden by the ferns. "Please, just go back to your berries."

Jake could no longer see the bear, but he knew the animal could still smell them. And was still watching. Waiting. Deciding what to do.

As far as Jake knew, black bear encounters were usually uneventful. But the way things had gone over the past two days, Jake should prepare for the worst. The bear out of sight, he turned and led Kelsey away from the coast, deeper into the woods.

Unfortunately, giving the bear a wide berth meant heading back in the direction they'd come from—at least for a little while.

"What about the men?" Kelsey asked again, stopping now and tugging her hand free. "We need to head away from them."

"And we will, Kelsey, as soon as possible. If it weren't for them, we'd keep our voices up so we'd scare off any other wildlife that might cause problems."

The deep ache in the back of his arm and across his chest grew worse, and he grimaced. If it became infected, he'd need some strong antibiotics and soon.

"Are you okay?" Kelsey blanched and stepped toward him. She reached out for his arm then caught herself. "I'm sorry, of course, you're not."

"I'm fine. Let's keep moving." Jake turned his back on her and hiked forward.

He wished he had a weapon to protect them. Seeing the bear magnified only one of their vulnerabilities—and like Kelsey said, they had to worry about the men following.

In truth, Jake was surprised they hadn't already been found. He fully expected they would be soon. But there was nothing more they could do except keep pressing forward.

Instead of a hard drenching rain, a mist fell, coating everything around them in a moist sheen. He trudged one foot in front of the other, Kelsey behind him, staying alert for their pursuers. A few minutes later he steered them north and back toward the coast.

A glance over his shoulder offered him reassurance that Kelsey was still there. He wanted to see her face, catch her eyes, a hint of a smile. But her head was down, watching the ground.

Her hair hung limp and wet beneath the hood of her jacket. She never looked up at him. He stumbled and turned his attention back to his steps. But his body, mind and heart, all of his senses, were keenly aware of her presence, listening to her cadence as she followed, to her breathing that told him she could use the exercise. Her heavy sighs that let him know of her frustration with their predicament.

Right now, he wished he could hear that little happy sigh she made sometimes. Or at least used to make. Not going to happen until they were far from here. Maybe not ever as far as he was concerned.

Bitter regret filled his mouth. Best to focus on surviving.

They followed a game trail now, same as the other animals, which meant they risked running into something. It was worth the risk, though, because better time could be made this way.

Jake figured they'd been hiking for an hour if not two. No sign of their pursuers. The trail began to steepen, thick with mud and rainwater runoff. Jake slipped a couple times. The clouds grew darker, but the mist stayed with them, not relinquishing control to an all-out rain.

Soaked to the bone like this, he doubted they could go on for another day before one or both of them started coming down with something. But maybe that was just his mother talking.

A hot bowl of chicken soup sounded good about now.

The crash of waves against the rocky shore resounded, letting him know they were close to the shoreline. But was there a beach they could walk for miles without risking getting caught between a headland and a high tide?

Jake took the next few steps and found himself hedging the rim of a sea cliff. Kelsey came to stand next to him and he pressed her behind him and eased back. "This ground's unstable from all the rain."

When he turned around, he saw someone lurking a few yards away behind the trees. Someone with an eye patch... and a look of pure murder on his face.

A guttural sound chilled Kelsey to the core. The bear again? But this sounded more...human.

All her thoughts flashed through her mind at the same instant that she whirled to face this new menace. Make that old threat. Ritter raced toward her and Jake. Behind them, the rock-faced one-hundred-foot drop into the ocean.

There wasn't anywhere to run. They were trapped.

"He's going to push us over." She braced herself.

"Get back." Jake shoved her out of the man's path. "Run, Kelsey!"

Jake rushed to meet him, barreling into him to force him back and give them some room to escape, but Ritter was bigger. Stronger.

And as they wrestled, grunted, the big jerk slowly forced Jake closer to the cliff.

Her knees shook. Heart pounded. *I have to help.*

She searched the ground for a rock small enough to pick up, big enough to do damage. Or a stick. Anything to help Jake fight.

The man reached inside his jacket and pulled out a gun. Apparently, he'd wanted this battle with Jake to be hand-to-hand combat, but now he feared he might lose and wanted to end it.

She jumped on his back and pulled his hair, but he threw her off. Air rushed from her lungs when she hit the ground, grateful this time for the rain-soaked mossy earth.

Kelsey sucked in a breath and climbed to her knees. Jake had a stronghold on him and forced him to release the gun. But he kept Jake from reaching it, and Kelsey couldn't get at it, either.

While Jake wrestled with 'him, she glanced at the woods behind them for the others. She couldn't believe Ritter was alone. Had they spread out in their search?

The man punched Jake's wounded arm, and he went down, groaning. Face red, his eyes watered and he held Kelsey's gaze—she could hardly stand to look at the desperation there. He'd wanted her to promise to leave him if it came to that.

He was begging her with his gaze to go now.

She shook her head, stepping back. No...

The man kicked Jake in the gut. Hard.

Then Ritter's attention fell on her.

She tugged out the map still wrapped in the protective plastic. "Take it. We don't want it."

His lip curled in a snarl as he took a step toward her. Kelsey backed away instinctively, even though she wanted him to have the map. "Just let us go."

He grabbed the gun as he moved toward her. "Can't do that. I'm supposed to bring just you and the map."

Just her? What about Jake?

The man chambered a round. "You know what that means."

It wasn't a question.

Tears blurred her vision. She didn't want to speak her fears aloud. "You can't."

"And why's that?" The smirk on his face sent shudders through her.

Jake got to his feet behind Ritter, but the guy's focus was still on her. Careful not to telegraph Jake's movement, giving him away, she kept her eyes focused on Ritter, hoping that Jake could somehow save himself.

And then...Jake slipped over the side of the sea cliff.

FOURTEEN

Kelsey screamed his name.

The sound gripped his heart and squeezed.

Against the slippery terrace, barely a foot in width, Jake clung to the lone root extended from the rough and mud-slicked face of the sea cliff. Pain lashed his arm, chest and gut. The gunshot had blasted through his left triceps, and that was the only reason he could hang on—anywhere else, and Jake would be at the bottom of the cliff now. But he still had limited use of both his arms.

He struggled to calm his breathing. Couldn't give himself away.

If Ritter came close enough to look, maybe the ground would give way where he stood, too. And then Kelsey would be safe. Sweat pouring down his back, despite the cool mist, he pressed his eyes shut and prayed.

God, please, please help us out of this. Show me what to do!

Seconds ticked by. Had the man taken Kelsey and disappeared into the woods without even a glimpse over the side? Jake gripped the root, wondering if he'd have enough strength to pull himself back up. Rocks crunched as footfalls approached.

He held his breath.

Crouched perfectly still.

Clenching the root, he prayed it would hold. Would Ritter see him there and try to kick the root loose or shoot Jake? How could Jake defend himself? How could he even begin to save Kelsey?

The man's chin edged over the cliff face. No more time to think.

Jake lunged upward to grab Ritter's boot. It was the only way.

Pebbles trickled by and then…more of the muddy rain-soaked earth collapsed. Jake held on to the root with everything in him and pressed himself into the muddy rocks like it was his only hope.

His only refuge.

Ritter let out a panicked bellow as the edge gave way and he slid down. Jake grabbed his arm, stopping him from the fall to his death.

He struggled to breathe. Why had he just saved Ritter?

Reflex. Pure reflex. And now, Jake stared down at the terror in Ritter's eyes.

Eyes that begged for mercy though they'd shown none. This man had been ready to kill Jake, and eventually Kelsey. And yet the guy wanted mercy? But how could Jake offer anything less?

He gripped the root with everything in him—the pain exploding from his arm and chest denying him. He groaned under Ritter's weight as he pulled with his right hand. But his palm and fingers were muddy. Slick.

And Ritter began to slide. The man grabbed on to the narrow strip of earth where Jake barely maintained his footing, and even that began to fail. Ritter's fingers skated over the terrace as he lost his grip.

Jake looked into Ritter's eyes, willing him to hang on. "Don't worry. I'm not going to let you go."

And he didn't. But Ritter slipped from his grasp all the same. The man's terrifying, hollow scream echoed as he

plummeted. The look on his face, in his eyes as he fell…
Jake squeezed his eyes shut.

Oh, God, I'm so sorry. Jake pressed his face against the
muddy cliff side and wept. *I'm so sorry.*

"Jake."

He allowed himself to gasp for breath now, unsure if he'd
ever get over what had just happened.

"Look at me," Kelsey said. Pleaded.

How could he ever look at another person without seeing
Ritter's face? Hearing his cry as he fell to his death?

He reined in his outburst before edging his gaze upward. Feeling the cold mist against his cheeks, he looked at
Kelsey—her eyes brimming with tears, her cheeks shimmer-
ing in the humidity. She was pressed against the ground, her
arms reaching for him.

What was she thinking?

"It's too dangerous," he said. "I can't watch you fall, too.
Get away."

He didn't know if he could climb back up. Now that he
thought about it, she might be better off leaving him behind.
But Jake wasn't ready to die just yet.

Too many things left unsettled.

He gripped the root again, knowing his hands would slip
on anything else—there was nothing but muddy, slippery
rocks on the sea cliff. Could he put his entire weight on this
lone root again?

Could he trust everything in him to God?

"Let me help you. I can pull you up." Kelsey reached forward, the tips of her finger barely reaching the top of his head
as he stood on the slim ledge.

He sucked in a couple of breaths. Got the oxygen going
to his muscles—what was left of them. Wrapping his hands
around the root he pulled, putting his entire weight onto it.
Please hold.

It shifted.

Pebbles and mud and dirt tumbled past him. He would be next.

"Give me your hand." Her tone wavered, threaded with desperation. With fear.

He gripped her moist palm—not much better traction than the rocks—and eased off the root. Just a little.

"Don't let me pull you over the side. If I'm too much, let go."

"I'm not letting go of you. Ever."

This wasn't the time, but their eyes met. Something passed between them.

He didn't need her promise that she would let go for her own safety this time. He would be the one, rather than take her with him.

His palm slipped in hers.

Just like Ritter's had in his.

"Jake, don't you let go of me."

He tugged on the root, planting his toes in the crevices, mustering his strength, clinging to the rocks. They threatened to toss him to his death on the sea-ravaged stones below, to be washed away in the salty water.

Muscles straining, Jake groaned and pulled himself up until his waist was level with the edge. The root gave way.

But Kelsey held. Tugging him forward, she fell on her backside as he crawled the rest of the way and collapsed.

She held on to him. Still hadn't let go.

"I told you—" she gasped for breath "—I wouldn't let go."

Jake's face pressed into the damp ground, dirt in his mouth. He lay still, breathing in the earthy scent. Grateful he hadn't lost his life. Regretting that he'd not been able to help Ritter.

He wanted to sleep a million years.

But in a soft, warm bed.

"And I told Ritter, I wouldn't let go." He closed his eyes, hating the image of Ritter's face, the sound of his scream as it played through his mind.

"Why'd you risk your life to try to save him?"

Jake opened his eyes. "Because," he croaked the word, "mercy trumps judgment." That was something his dad had taught him before he'd died, but Jake didn't dare bring up his father now. Kelsey would only start thinking about hers.

Kelsey held her face near his. "I thought I lost you back there, twice."

His chuckle was more like a gasp. And it sounded insane. He was going crazy.

She pressed her forehead against his temple, her warm breath fanning his cheek. "Don't ever do that again."

"What? You don't want me to jump off another cliff for you?" Jake rolled onto his back, a few rocks gouging into him even in the soft moss, but he was too exhausted to care at the moment. Too enamored with Kelsey, the look in her eyes, the longing expression on her face. Would he hear that little happy sigh now?

Her gazed pressed him. "I'm serious."

"I didn't do it on purpose. Not like I could have controlled what happened." The story of his life. No control whatsoever.

A soft smile lifted her lips. "Jake…"

His insides stoked, despite his dead-tired, battle-weary body. Maybe it would be enough to get him through. To boost his energy reserves. He smiled back and squeezed her arm, hiding how terrified he was that while they'd triumphed over this obstacle, they wouldn't make it out of this alive.

That had been close.

Too close.

Kelsey climbed to her feet and watched Jake scrape his battered body from the cold ground. He reached for his left arm again, lifting the jacket this time to look.

Oh, no. He was bleeding again. Across his chest, too.

"Jake," she whispered.

His frown-laden gaze drew up to meet hers. She thought

he might say something. Instead he tried to smile but it faltered. He lifted his good arm, and she went to him, hugging
him close. The coppery smell of the fresh blood on his shirt
accosted her. She turned her face away, unwilling to look.

She pressed her forehead against his chest. What were
they going to do? When she lifted her face, Jake studied the
forest. Looking for the others? Or trying to decide on their
best route? When he glanced down at her, his face was close.

So close.

"Kelsey," he whispered.

The sound of her name on his lips brought a rush of memories—the good kind that wrapped around you and left you
floating and warm. That nearly did her in.

She'd never stopped loving him, and the fact that she'd let
him slip away ripped at her heart. She didn't want to let another minute go. If only she could trust him this time.

But to say her thoughts now…her heart stuttered. She had
to try.

"About you and me. If we make it out of this," she said.
"Do you think we—"

"Shh." He pressed a finger against her lips. To silence her?
Keep her from asking if he would give her a second chance?
Them a second chance?

Then she realized he was listening to something other
than her.

She squeezed his arm. "What is it?"

"Come on." He grabbed her hand and trudged forward. His
form looked beaten and strong at the same time.

Deeper into the woods, he led her—the green old-growth
forest an incredible sight she'd love to see any other time. But
she wasn't on a pleasure trip or even a writing assignment.

With that thought, Davis's face filled her vision, blurring
out the vegetation around her. Her decision to accept the position he had offered had led her into this. But if she wasn't

here with Jake right now, then maybe someone else would be instead.

He trudged deeper into the thick canopy.

"I thought you planned to hug the coast," she whispered.

Squeezing her hand, he sent her a warning look.

Keep silent.

He wasn't even willing to risk speaking himself.

What seemed like hours later, Kelsey's legs ached and she didn't think she could take another step. On the other hand, the hike hadn't been as difficult as he'd made it sound when he'd said they would have to climb rocks along the coast. Running into Ritter had obviously changed his mind about going that way.

She'd wanted to ask him about it, but he'd demanded silence. A clear rain-swollen stream rushed over green rocks and Jake hesitated before crossing over. "You thirsty?"

"Can we drink it?"

"Maybe. Maybe not. You could probably drink rainwater caught in the leaves or something. I don't know." His pale face sent fear down her spine.

"You should sit. You need to rest." She hated the tremble in her voice.

He shook his head, defiant. "I'm afraid I won't be able to get back up."

It was that bad?

Kelsey rubbed her arms, and allowed her gaze to drift to a lone cedar among a copse of old spruce trees—at anything but Jake.

I will not cry. I will not cry.

"Come here," he said.

Kelsey went to him and snuggled into his arms. If only she felt completely secure there, but something was wrong. He was burning up, for one thing.

"How much farther until we find help?" she asked, but doubted he had an answer.

There was something he wasn't telling her. Was his wound infected? She hadn't know it could happen so fast. Regardless, she could feel it in his body heat. Sense it in his demeanor. He knew it, too. Was he about to give up? Tell her to go on without him?

"Jake, let's pray. Like we did before."

He squeezed tighter, but didn't answer.

Okay, if he couldn't answer, she'd take that as a yes. "Lord, please be our Guiding Light. Guide us to civilization. To help. Protect us from those men who want the map. Who want to kill us. Forgive me for taking it to begin with." *And keep Jake alive. Keep him...with me.*

Oh, Lord, we need help!

Jake released his hold on her. "We'd better get going. Drink if you're going to drink."

Kelsey noticed a pocket of leaves filled with mist and rainwater. Probably safer than drinking the stream water and risking giardia. She'd heard often enough that there wasn't any safe water these days, even in the wilderness. She allowed herself a few drops then offered the rest to Jake. Despite the cold sweat beading on his brow.

They weren't going to make it. He wasn't going to make it.

Pulse thrumming wildly in her neck, her breath caught in her throat.

He drank the rest of the water, like a man desperate to douse the flames. A man who knew it wouldn't be enough.

Jake took two steps forward and collapsed.

FIFTEEN

Kelsey dropped to her knees next to Jake. Disbelief constricted her chest.

She laid her palms against his hot cheeks and turned his face toward her. "Jake, wake up."

Her mind screamed. *Please be all right.*

Her heart cried out to God. *Why won't You help us?*

She pressed her forehead to his and squeezed her eyes shut, willing him to open his. To be all right. Jake was a strong man. An athlete, even. And to see him like this…something inside Kelsey broke. She closed her eyes tight against a torrent of emotion, pressure squeezing her heart and head.

What did she do now? How could she help him? Kelsey tugged his shoulder forward and attempted to lift him so she could carry him like a fireman would. But it was no use—his muscular frame was too heavy. She eased him back, making sure his head rested against a soft mossy spot.

Kelsey looked up and studied the woods. She was helpless. Alone.

And terrified. Somehow, she had to get Jake out of here. This was up to her now.

The woods were quiet. Too quiet. Except for the sound of water tumbling over pebbles and rocks.

The stream. Kelsey knelt closer, feeling moisture seep into her jeans at the knees, and cupped her hands so that the icy water could pool. Then she held her hands over Jake's face and allowed water to trickle between her fingers and wash over his forehead and cheeks, hoping he'd regain consciousness.

Nothing.

Not even a flinch. Kelsey shoved to her feet and stared ahead at the direction they'd been hiking. Jake had wanted her to promise to leave him. Obviously, he'd feared this would happen.

"What am I going to do?" She pressed the heels of her palms into her eyes. "I can't leave you."

I can't.

Then again, if she didn't, he wouldn't have a chance of getting help.

She reached down and grabbed him under the arms, dragging him away from the stream to a tree where he might be better protected. But…he was heavy. This survival stuff wasn't her thing.

Jake groaned.

Kelsey's heart jumped. "Jake?"

But he didn't respond to her voice. She released him gently to rest, his back cushioned by fern fronds against a tree.

A branch snapped behind her.

She whirled to see a man dressed in camouflaged hiking gear and a ski mask. She gasped. He tugged the mask off, revealing a thick silver beard and hair, and unfamiliar lined features.

Was he with Lennon and Flanagan? He took a step forward.

She stood in front of Jake in a ridiculous effort to hide him. "What do you want?"

Her heart lurched. Maybe he wasn't dangerous. Maybe he was a hiker like Jake had hoped they'd run into. Someone to help.

He studied her, then his gaze drifted to the ground behind

her where it lingered for a few seconds. Lifting his hand, he gestured at Jake. "What are you going to do about him?"

How much should she tell this man? She was completely defenseless. At his mercy. "He needs help. I was going to leave him and find someone who could help."

He frowned and took a step back.

Though her gut swirled in warning, Kelsey moved toward him. She wasn't sure if she could trust him. But what choice did she have? "Please, can you help us? Do you have a cell phone I could use?"

He shook his head. The guy was giving her the creeps.

"Then maybe you can hike down and get someone who can help us."

"No." He moved toward Kelsey.

Every muscle in her body tensed. She glanced around for a stick. A rock—something to defend herself with.

"Don't worry," he said. "I'm not going to hurt you."

He skirted her and bent over Jake to examine his wounds. "I was afraid it would come to this."

"What? Come to what? Who are you?"

Ignoring her, the guy lifted Jake and carried him just like Kelsey had tried and failed. He trudged off, leaving her standing there.

She bolted after him. "Wait. Where are you taking him?"

But the guy didn't answer. Kelsey followed, sensing that he meant to help, even though he was a little off. The deeper into the woods and the farther from the coastline he hiked, the more Kelsey's concern grew. Finally, she rushed to stand in front of him, which wasn't easy considering his long gait.

"I need you to tell me right now where you're taking him."

Breathing hard, she could see the strain on his features as he shoved right by her. Then in the thicket, he pulled back a dense layer of ivy, revealing an old, wobbly cedar door. A black widow spider crawled from the ivy he'd disturbed, and he thumped it away then walked through the door and disappeared.

Kelsey drew in a long breath and shoved through the ivy, feeling like she was in an *Indiana Jones* movie. Only this adventure was anything but entertaining.

Stepping over the threshold, she entered a small, dimly lit room. Blinking a few times as her eyes adjusted, she took in the cozy setting—a couple overstuffed chairs and sofa on a rug—and watched the man lay Jake on a double bed against the wall.

"You *live* here?" She thought they were in a wilderness area, or national park or something. Didn't think anyone was allowed to live there.

Kelsey approached Jake and laid her hand across his forehead, a gesture that reminded her of her mother when Kelsey was sick. Jake definitely had a fever. He had to be seriously ill to be unconscious like this. She sat on the bed next to him and glanced around the room, hating that she was at this odd man's mercy. Hoping and praying that he would provide their desperately needed help.

He'd disappeared again. A small fire in a potbellied stove warmed the room and enveloped Kelsey. A few pictures of the man with his army friends covered the walls.

Her stomach growled. She ignored her body's needs, her attention on Jake and what to do for him.

Suddenly, he gripped her arm and sat up. His panic-stricken, bloodshot eyes stared at her. "Where are we?"

Kelsey put all her energy into forcing him back down. "Someone is helping us, Jake. Just rest."

God, please let this man help Jake and then get us out of here. With the thought, she realized that Lennon and Flanagan could still be following them. With Jake's condition, she'd almost forgotten their other predicament.

The man returned, entering from a door in the opposite wall. He assembled an IV stand.

"What are you doing?" Kelsey jumped to her feet.

"Taking care of your friend."

This guy was a hermit and reminded her of an old, worn-out war veteran with his fatigues. "Were you a medic in the army?"

"Something like that."

Kelsey watched him attach the IV and in a few moments, Jake was receiving the fluid, hopefully with antibiotics. After that, he cleaned Jake's wound and put on a new bandage. All good, but Kelsey was still worried.

"Can you tell me…what? What's wrong with him?"

He slid his thick fingers down his beard and studied her like she was an idiot for not knowing. "You tell me."

"Well, he's been shot. He's lost blood." *A lot of blood.* "We haven't eaten in a…maybe a couple days." She'd leave out that he'd been beaten up by the men and nearly drowned. She hadn't told him about them yet. "He's exhausted."

The man nodded. "Don't forget you've been hiking for a couple days now. I suspect the adrenaline rush that kept him going this long finally crashed. It's a total load thing. And now he's got a fever. So we're going to fix him up. Get rid of the infection before it can turn septic if it hasn't already."

Septic? She swallowed, grateful to the stranger who'd given Jake antibiotics. That could mean his life. She owed him an explanation.

"What's your name?" Kelsey held her breath, thinking that maybe she shouldn't have asked.

"Eric." He opened the door of the potbellied stove, allowing the firelight to send shadows dancing across the room. She watched them skate over Jake's face.

For the first time she thought about the fire. Would the escaping smoke give away their location?

She needed to warn Eric about the dangerous men after them. What would happen once she did? Would he toss her and Jake out before Jake was ready and leave them to find their own way to civilization?

Kelsey rubbed her temples. Tired, hungry and scared, she didn't know if she should tell him now or wait. But what if she waited and he wasn't prepared if and when Lennon and Flanagan found them?

This guy was so seriously hidden away, she doubted that would happen anytime soon.

"I need to tell you there are dangerous men following us."

He stoked the fire in the stove then turned his gaze on her. "I know."

"What do you—" Her spirits sank to the floor. "You're one of them, aren't you?"

That's where Lennon had intended to go this whole time—to meet this man tucked away in the wilderness.

He poured steaming liquid into cups and handed one to her. Wary, Kelsey took the cup, but she wouldn't drink.

"Don't worry, it's just coffee. And no, I'm not with those men after you."

"Then how did you—"

"I've been following you. Ever since you came into my woods."

My woods? "Following us?"

"I had hoped you'd keep going and make it out all on your own. But since you didn't, I don't need anyone coming here to look for you."

"You mean you don't need anyone finding *you*." Kelsey wished she hadn't spoken the words. "I promise, we won't tell anyone where you are, or that you're even here."

"You're right. You won't."

An arctic chill belied the warm, cozy feel of the room and raced down her spine. She glanced at the cup, unwilling to drink from it. Then at Jake. What had the man really given him?

"If I was going to hurt you, I would have let those men find you. They were bearing down on you as it was."

He really had been watching them. Kelsey thought Jake had sensed someone—but she assumed it was the men coming for the map. But this man, Eric, was near the whole time, stalking them, watching them. Kelsey frowned, hating the disturbing sensations flooding her.

She eyed him over the rim of her cup as she took her first sip of warm liquid, watching for any sign that he'd drugged the brew. This crazy situation was making her paranoid. He smiled, causing her to tip her cup away from her lips.

"Here, you can drink from mine if you don't trust me." He thrust his cup forward.

She'd seen him pour the liquid in both cups. "No, that's okay."

He tugged a chair out from the small table. "Sit here. I'll fix us something to eat. When your friend wakes up, he'll be hungry, too. Then when you're rested, I'll show you out. That is, if you agree you won't tell anyone about me or where I live."

And what if she didn't agree? No way would she voice that question. Besides, Kelsey couldn't imagine finding her way back. "I promise, I won't say anything in exchange for your help."

While Eric worked, Kelsey's eyes fell on his Bible, lying open on the rustic table.

The LORD is my shepherd, I shall not want. He makes me lie down in green pastures; He leads me beside quiet waters.

He restores my soul… Your rod and Your staff, they comfort me…

When, God? Because I'm sure not feeling any comfort right now. But then again, she was here in this seemingly safe place.

Keeping this man's secret—it was the least she could do. But…

Trust a stranger?

Kelsey had no choice but to trust this man. But what reason did he have to trust her to keep his secret?

Jake opened his eyes.

The room was dark except for the glow of embers through
the opened door of the woodstove.

He rubbed his face, trying to remember where he was.
What had happened? Soft snoring told him he wasn't alone
in the room. He shifted on the bed, hating the squeak, and
spotted Kelsey on the too-short couch. She had to be uncomfortable in that position. Jake wanted to trade with her, let her
have the bed. Disturbing her sleep at the moment probably
wasn't a good idea, though.

A large, bulky form nestled under blankets on the rug. His
face was a blurred image in Jake's mind at the moment—but
Jake knew he owed the man. Jake vaguely recalled Kelsey
telling him about their situation and the man who'd rescued
them—an old war veteran hermit, she'd called him.

Jake sighed, feeling much better. Like a completely new
man. He reached up to feel his wound and found it ban-
daged—he couldn't remember anything of that. But he did
remember eating a gamy soup.

And Kelsey's concerned face, her soothing voice coax-
ing the liquid and a few chunks of meat he didn't recognize
between his lips. She'd whispered words to him, probably
suspecting that he wouldn't hear her, but maybe at the same
time, hoping he would.

The words drifted back to him from somewhere in his
subconscious.

Jake, I...I love you. Don't leave me.

From those words, he'd found the strength and the will he
needed to pull out of his fever. He was sure they had made
all the difference. He'd needed to hear them.

He needed something else, too. Something he'd never heard

her say. What he really needed to hear from her was that she could trust him. She *would* trust him. Believe in him.

He wouldn't leave her—but he wanted to *know* that she wouldn't leave him, this time. If there was a *this time*. He glanced over at Kelsey again, then sat up, dizziness washing over him in waves.

The form on the floor stirred and started mumbling. Jake didn't know how to thank the man who'd been there for them; despite the help, he still made Jake uneasy. No one lived in these woods like this, unless they didn't want to be found. That gave Jake a disturbing feeling in his gut.

Tension knotted his shoulders. How long had they been here already? Had his brother finally gotten suspicious and sent help?

Jake swiped a hand down his face, feeling his unshaven jaw. By the thicker growth he could tell he'd been out of it a couple days, at least, maybe more. Lying back down to get some rest might be a good idea, but definitely, they should leave tomorrow.

They had a long hike ahead of them.

With the thought, an image of Ritter's face came to mind. Falling, screaming. Jake shifted in the bed and forced his thoughts elsewhere.

The form on the floor twitched. His mumbling, emotional and frantic, grew louder. Jake feared it would wake Kelsey. But there wasn't anything he could do. His hands clasped together, Jake sank into the pillow. If this man hadn't shown up, Jake might have died. Kelsey, too. But while they'd been rescued, they still weren't safe. This wasn't over yet.

Those men would never give up on finding Kelsey until they had the map she'd taken. Maybe this guy could show them the quickest route to the nearest town and sheriff. They could tell him everything, hand over the map and be done with it. Jake could only hope and pray that it would be that easy.

The mumbling grew louder, more coherent. Though he didn't want to eavesdrop, something in the man's words sounded ominous. Jake inched off the pillow, listening.

"Can't let them leave... They'll ruin everything. Shouldn't have brought them."

Rigid, Jake sat up now, hearing dread in the man's voice. *He can't let us leave?*

SIXTEEN

"Kelsey."

A pleasant, familiar voice whispered her name. She snuggled deeper into the dream with Jake.

A nudge on her shoulder startled her.

Kelsey frowned, not wanting her dream disturbed, but she opened her eyes, squinting, struggling to wake up.

A man crouched next to her on the sofa. Kelsey drew in a breath and a hand clamped over her mouth.

"Shh," Jake whispered. Confusion tumbled through her thoughts. What was going on?

He pressed his mouth next to her ear and spoke so low, she could barely make out the words. "We have to get out of here."

She jerked back and shook her head. How did she make him understand? They were safe, for the most part. Jake had to get stronger. Eric could be trusted. He would lead them to a town. But Jake kept his hand pressed against her lips, his eyes pleading.

Her spirits took a dive. Jake was delirious. She'd thought he was getting better.

Eric stirred and Kelsey hoped he'd wake up to help her. Jake's grip on her was strong as he kept them both completely still. Quiet. Eric settled back into a fitful sleep, mumbling something about keeping them here.

Shock coursed through her. She locked eyes with Jake.

Now she understood. She nodded her agreement, but how would they gather their jackets and put on their shoes without waking him?

Then…which way would they go? Away from one crazy person only to be ambushed by other crazy people? Kelsey rubbed her eyes.

The LORD is my shepherd.

Jake's gaze roamed over her face, taking in her features like he hadn't seen her in years. There wasn't time for this. He looked away—though what she'd seen in his eyes had been brief, she hadn't missed it. She held on to the warmth his yearning had stoked.

Jake stood, his movements easy, quiet. But he wasn't trained in stealth like Eric. He crept across the floor and Kelsey followed, praying the boards didn't creak and give them away.

He leads me beside quiet waters.

This was impossible.

Eric would wake up.

But then she remembered he'd had a few beers. More than a few, in fact. She'd been afraid of what he might do, but he only ended up sharing about his war experiences. Kelsey had finally snuggled onto the sofa while she listened to his long, sorrowful tales. Finally the tales had transformed into a peaceful contentment as he talked about how he'd found God, though he still struggled with drinking.

The next thing she knew, Jake crouched next to the sofa where she slept.

Now he tugged their jackets from a hook by the door and handed them to Kelsey. He lifted their shoes, and handed her pair over. When he shook his head, she took that to mean they should wait to put them on. At the door, he fumbled with the lock. The door clicked.

Freezing, they both glanced at Eric. He didn't stir, but he'd stopped mumbling. Maybe he would wake up soon.

They had to hurry. With one last glance around the small cozy room that had been their shelter for a few days, Kelsey noticed that Jake had left his bed to appear like he was still in it, puffing up the pillows. She'd slept in the small bedroom the past few days and had only fallen asleep on the sofa last night, listening to Eric's stories, so at first glance Eric might believe she was back in the bedroom.

For someone who had been out of it for days, Jake had it together now. Much more than she did. He cracked the door enough for them to slip through. Ivy crawled over her and she shoved images of spiders from her mind, trailing Jake through into the cold night air. With care, he pressed the door closed. Moonlight barely penetrated the canopy, but it was enough for her to see Jake's chest rise and fall with his relieved sigh. Eric's alcohol consumption had kept him slumbering while she and Jake escaped.

Kelsey moved to put on her shoes, but Jake held her back. "Not yet," he whispered.

Great. Kelsey couldn't stand the thought of tromping through this wilderness in her bare feet. Jake eyed her. He handed his shoes to her.

Kelsey frowned but took them, wondering what he would do next. Jake's strong arms swooped under her legs as he lifted her and started hiking. Smiling, she pressed her face against his shoulder to stifle the giggle she felt bubbling inside.

The man's strength, after everything he'd been through, amazed her.

"I can walk, you know," she whispered against his neck. "You're not strong enough and this could break your wound open again. You don't need to waste your energy on me."

He ignored her, leaving her last words to hang between them, and shuffled through and over the greenery until he tucked them behind a large spruce. She thought he would put her down now, but he held her closer. In the darkness, Kelsey inched her face up to his, feeling his breath against her cheek.

Her breathing quickened as she pressed her hand against his unshaven jaw. "I thought I would lose you. How many times are you going to make me go through that?"

"Apparently, I'm hard to be rid of." He set her on her feet, slicing open the moment.

Disappointment swept through her that he hadn't met her halfway. Hadn't kissed her. She followed his lead and slipped on her shoes, blinking back the stinging tears. She felt like a little girl. A stupid little girl. For a while on *The Buccaneer,* she thought they'd grown closer—even in the midst of danger—but something had happened to change him.

Was it their past coming between them again? She'd hurt him badly before. He wouldn't forget so easily. Nor could she trust so easily.

Jake got his shoes on first. "We have to make good time. We don't know when he'll discover we're gone, or what he'll do when he does. We need to be far away."

"If he decides to pursue us, we don't stand much chance. He's been following us since we entered what he termed were *his* woods. But I think we can trust him. He's one of the good guys."

"I'm not so sure." Jake's tone turned gruff. "Let's put some distance between us."

Kelsey shoved away from the tree and stood in a patch of moonlight. Jake hated seeing that hurt look in her eyes. Hated that he'd put it there. He'd wanted to kiss her just now, but this wasn't the time.

When he told her how he felt about her, it would be when she was ready to hear it. When she was ready to trust him. When she was ready to play for keeps. He couldn't bear it otherwise.

Still, it was all he could do to resist her now, vulnerable and needing the reassurance a shared kiss would bring.

His better judgment gave in to his heart. He cupped her cheek and leaned closer, pressing his mouth against her soft lips. These past months without her exploded in a torrent of emotion as he deepened the kiss. He savored her softness, her sweetness and slid his hands up her neck to weave his fingers through her hair and bring her closer.

She trembled, but whether from his kiss or from cold or fear of what would happen next, he couldn't know.

A crashing noise resounded through the trees.

Jake stiffened, the kiss broken.

"Come on." He grabbed her hand and ran as fast as he could, mindful of Kelsey behind him. They darted through the undergrowth and between the trees, over and under fallen trunks, his vision straining at times in the dark canopy.

Morning would be on them soon enough. If their pursuers were still hunting them, they could spot Jake and Kelsey, as well. It worked both ways. But this time Jake was more prepared, and he wasn't suffering from an open, bleeding wound. He would have plenty of time for a full recovery once they made it home.

Behind him, Kelsey yelped and her hand slipped from his. He spun to find her on the ground.

"Are you okay?" He kept his voice low.

"Yes, sorry. I tripped."

He assisted her to her feet and gripped her shoulder to look in her face. "We have to give this everything we've got, okay? Run as fast, as long and as hard as we can. Are you with me?"

She gave a slight nod.

He held his hand out and she grabbed it, squeezing. Good. Together, they just might survive. Jake turned on his heel and continued trudging toward the coast. Somewhere in the canopy, he spotted the gray light of dawn edging into the forest. And he smelled the ocean.

There was no way for him to know if the men were still searching for the map. He could only hope they'd given up on their search, fixed *The Buccaneer* and were far away by now, but Jake couldn't take the risk.

"We're headed to the coastline again?" she asked.

Jake slowed up to hike next to her, and kept his voice low. "That's the only way for me to get any bearing on our location."

The dark blue of the salty water peeked through the trees, and Jake slowed at the edge of the forest, not wanting to give himself away if the wrong people were still hunting them. He remembered too well what happened the last time he stood at the edge of a sea cliff. From here, he could see the coastline and hoped he would see the coast guard or a marine patrol searching for them.

But he saw nothing but a wall of marine fog.

Despite his disappointment at not finding a search and rescue party, he was still relieved that he didn't see *The Buccaneer*.

He tugged out the map from his back pocket that he'd snagged from Eric's cabin.

Kelsey gasped. "You have a map?"

"I took it from our friend. I'm sorry, I had no choice. He knows his way around and we don't. We could die without a map. I wish we could have thanked him. Wished he would have led us to civilization. But we couldn't risk it. You understand, right?"

Her misty hazel eyes grew wide.

"What is it?"

She dug through her jacket, feeling around in the pockets. "The map! He took the map."

Whirling around, she headed into the forest again.

"Are you kidding me?" Jake grabbed her arm. "You are not going back there for it." He doubted she could find her way even if she wanted to try.

She stomped the ground. "I can't believe I didn't notice it was gone. I didn't even think about it."

"You should be glad you left it. That thing has done nothing but put our lives in danger for the last few days. A map we didn't even know existed until this all started. Crazy the lengths people will go to for money."

"You mean like you grabbing *The Buccaneer* as part of your job?"

Whoa. Where did that come from? Neither one of them were at their best at the moment. He let her comment slide and focused on the map of the Olympic Wilderness. He followed the coastline with his finger starting from where he thought they'd docked. But the map wasn't precision perfect when depicting the rocky shores.

In fact, it could be as off as he was when it came to relationships.

Soon Kelsey stood next to him, looking at the map, too. She pressed her finger and pointed to a place miles into the interior and away from the coastline. "There. I didn't see it before, when he took us to his hiding place, but I see it now. There's the little stream and we walked this way."

Slowly, she lifted her gaze to meet his. "I know where he is."

"There are a lot of little streams like that. But it doesn't matter. You're not going back." He hoped he wouldn't have to fight her on this. He sure didn't want to remind her that it was because she'd taken the map to begin with that they were still being hunted.

"I promised him I wouldn't tell anyone where he lived, or even that he was there, if he helped us. If he helped you."

"Then keep your promise."

"I didn't think I could find my way back so I didn't worry about it."

"If the guy has any sense, he packed up his stuff and is long gone by now. His hiding place has been discovered."

"We don't really know what he meant when he was talking in his sleep. We don't know if he would have acted on it. He helped us, Jake. It feels wrong that we left him like that. Does he even know that having the map puts him in danger?"

Jake shook his head. "He knows. He saw the way the men came after us. But he seems like the kind who knows how to take care of himself. We have to focus on our own safety."

Kelsey shivered. Without the trees to hold back the brisk wind, they were both getting colder. Jake shrugged out of his jacket.

"What are you doing?"

"Here. You're cold."

"You need your jacket the same as I need mine. Besides, if you get sick again…"

He frowned. What if she was right? What if he wasn't ready yet and ended up on the ground again? He shook his head. "I'm good now. You saved me, Kelsey. Take my jacket."

Staring at him, she refused.

"I'm not going to get sick again. I got antibiotics, remember? It's you I'm worried about. I promise, if I get cold, I'll let you know."

"You're sure you're not cold now?"

"I've been hiking and worked up a sweat. You take it." He thrust it toward her again, hoping she couldn't see through his words.

She grabbed it and slipped it on over her light jacket then wrapped her arms around herself. Jake wanted to assist her in that, but he shouldn't get distracted.

The map grew damp in the mist. Jake made his best guess and followed the coastline. "There. That's our town. We're heading for Hood."

"Jake?"

Something in Kelsey's tone sent dread through his soul.

He looked where Kelsey pointed at the marine fog clinging to the coast a few miles out.

The Buccaneer.

SEVENTEEN

Kelsey scrambled next to Jake into the darker edges of the forest. "Do you think they spotted us?"

"I don't know, but let's plan for the worst. They probably know where we're headed and want to beat us there."

"And wait for us?"

He didn't comment as he kept hiking, hugging the coast along the tree line.

Kelsey kept pace with him. "So we're still going to the town?"

"We don't have a choice."

"We can't win this race."

"No, but we can be smart about it. We can avoid being seen or caught while we try to get help so they can't stop or prevent us."

Images of the last time they'd sought out the sheriff surfaced in her mind. The gleaming knife pressed against Jake's neck. They had to make it within the walls of safety of the local law enforcement this time.

Jake increased his pace and Kelsey worked to keep up, but too soon, she started to tire. Her breaths got shorter, and an ache grew in her chest. She hadn't suffered as much as Jake yet she lagged behind.

You can do this.

They had to make it

I fear no evil, for You are with me...

The verses from Psalm 23 had been running through her mind since she'd read them from Eric's Bible. He was a troubled man, but from his stories, she knew he'd made his peace with God. She struggled to believe that he would harm them. Maybe he hadn't taken the map, either. Maybe it had simply fallen from her jacket.

She took another step and her foot lodged in a hole. Kelsey pivoted forward, sending pain shooting up her ankle. She sank to the ground. Really? Like they needed one more thing to happen.

In an instant, Jake was at her side. "Here. Let me see."

He gently lifted her ankle and tugged down her sock to reveal that swelling had already started. Then he set her foot gently against a green-slicked rock. He frowned and glanced up, taking in their surroundings, a look of hopelessness on his face.

Kelsey leaned her head back against a fallen trunk and gazed at the canopy. The musty smell of the lush old-growth forest would stay with her for days after this was over, she was sure. And the dark woods seemed to be closing in on them. With the way things were going, she wouldn't be shocked if Lennon and Flanagan stepped from behind a tree.

Jake sank to the ground next to her and hung his head. She'd watched him do that too often. When he lifted his head, his eyes caressed her face. He scooted closer.

"Come here," he said.

Kelsey had long ago grown accustomed to these words, his way of comforting her. She leaned into him, trying to forget the pain in her ankle. Forget their predicament. His masculine scent wrapped around her along with his strong arms, reassuring her in ways she wouldn't expect. She could fall asleep against him. Right here. Right now.

He rubbed her back and took a few breaths. Kelsey lifted her face to study him. "What are you thinking?" she asked.

He grinned. How could he grin at a time like this? And yet, she adored that grin. She envisioned them sitting on the deck of a boat in a warmer climate, sun beating down on his tanned face, and…that grin.

"I'm thinking that we've been chased, abducted, chased again, forced into a standoff with a bear. I've been shot and faced infection. Certain death. And then a crazy hermit. Now your ankle is sprained." He chuckled and looked into the woods. "Everything has to get better from here, right? We're going to make it, Kelsey."

He stood and offered his hand.

"How am I going to walk? No. You go get help. I'll wait right here."

"Do you trust me?"

She looked up at him, his gaze searching, pleading. His question seemed strange given the circumstances, but she knew from where it stemmed. Doubts crept into her thoughts. She didn't have an answer for what he was really asking, not long-term. But for now, she lifted her hand and gripped his.

Maybe she could do this. For him.

He tugged her up, and like he'd done once before, hefted her into his arms.

She gasped. "Jake, no, you can't carry me like this. Not the rest of the way."

"Wanna bet?" A dimple crept into his half smile.

Did he honestly believe they were going to make it? Kelsey wished she could tap into the hope he emanated. And, she wanted to trust him this time. Completely.

She hated how hard Jake worked to carry her. Though he tried to hide any strain he might feel, she felt his muscles tensing, working overtime, and could hear his breathing grow heavier.

Guilt accosted her. "It would be easier for you to carry me in a fireman's carry."

"Not for you it wouldn't." He didn't even look at her.

"What about piggyback?"

"Maybe in a bit."

Did he feel uncomfortable holding her like this? So close? Or was he simply trying to pay attention to where he stepped?

He worked his way up an incline. Even though the air was chilled and mist had morphed into a light rain, sweat poured from his temples, down his neck.

Kelsey hated herself for hurting her ankle, hated seeing him labor so hard for her.

"Okay, Jake. Enough. Put me down."

He lunged one last step up and topped the incline, and to her surprise, he gently set her on a stump and bent over to catch his breath, glancing up at her. "Don't think I'm this out of shape. I'm just not completely recovered from the gunshot."

Men. She shook her head. "I know that. I don't think you're a wimp, if that's what you're worried about." In fact, he was far from it.

Telling him what she really thought, at least when he was awake and coherent, was a little difficult for her. But he deserved to hear her admiration. Kelsey opened her mouth to speak—

"Look," he said and pointed. "Over there."

From where she sat, she couldn't see much without standing. She pushed up.

"Here," Jake said and hoisted her from the stump to stand on her good foot.

Nestled at the mouth of a river was a small town. They'd made it. Well, sort of. The fog hugged the coastline and hid part of the town. The marina wasn't even visible.

She turned her gaze to meet his.

"We have to think this through carefully," he said. "They could be headed this way to cut us off."

Jake sighed. They had to hurry, which was a total joke. They might even do better to circle around, but that was out of the question with Kelsey's ankle. Their options were cut-and-dried.

Jake didn't want to admit that he was feeling a little dizzy. "You ready?" he asked.

Shadows underscored her stunning hazel eyes, and exaggerated the atypical pallor of her skin. He couldn't wait to see some color back in her face. Jake reached up and ran his thumb down her cheek before he thought better of it.

She tensed. Jake looked away. He didn't need the rejection.

"I think a better question is, are you ready?" She frowned. "You're the one who has to carry me."

Doesn't matter. He shrugged.

Head, guts…no. He'd made it this far without having to dig deep, propel himself onward with his heart and soul. Maybe this was the end of the race.

Without giving it another thought, he lifted her slender form, settling her against him. How he'd love to do this at a time when they weren't in survival mode. A gust of wind blew her hair into his face. She swiped it from his eyes and in his peripheral vision, he caught her smile.

He smiled, too, without looking at her, his focus on descending the lush, green, slippery hill. At least he didn't have to descend a thirty-foot rock cliff.

But this would definitely be slow going.

Once they made it to the edge of what was beginning to look less like a town than he'd first thought, they'd have to make a beeline for the sheriff's office, if there even was one.

Exiting the woods into a grassy meadow, Kelsey tugged herself free and stood next to him. He wasn't ready to let her go. Not yet. And the reason had nothing at all to do with her ankle.

"You can help me walk the rest of the way, okay?" Expectation infused her voice.

Attagirl. "Okay."

He wrapped his arm under hers and assisted her loping

walk. They moved slower than he would have liked. If their assailants were anywhere near, Kelsey and Jake would have no chance of escape.

None.

He scanned the area in front of them and the perimeter, looking for their pursuers. If they were caught, they'd be in even deeper this time, because they'd taken the map with them, but had left it along the way. Even if Lennon believed their story, telling him what happened would put Eric at risk.

But Jake shoved the doubts behind him. They were going to make it. He wouldn't go down without a fight. They drew closer to the few buildings that made up the town, and when their feet hit concrete, Kelsey increased her pace.

Both of them felt the sense of urgency. They'd survived the wilderness and made it to civilization. But they were on a race against the men after the map. Finding someone to help them here could be their last chance. As they walked, they searched for a sheriff or deputy. Where were they when you needed them?

Across the way, Jake spotted the small substation sharing a building with a fish and tackle shop. He glanced both ways and they trudged across the street, a car slowing to let them cross. A few people stopped to watch, but no one offered assistance. In their bedraggled state, he and Kelsey must look like trouble.

He grinned and said hello to a few passersby.

Then…they stood at the door to the sheriff's office. Kelsey placed her hand on the knob and turned. The door swung open.

Jake assisted her into an empty room where she eased into the only chair on this side of a small desk. He glanced behind him, burying his disappointment. With no one there, he still didn't feel safe. But the men after the map wouldn't dare follow them into the sheriff's office.

A deputy stepped through the door at the back of the room.

"Can I help you?" he asked while looking them up and down. "Looks like you've been through the wringer."

"That's putting it mildly," Jake said.

"You in need of medical attention?"

Now there's a loaded question. He hadn't considered how to explain everything that had happened in a lucid fashion.

Kelsey placed her hands on the worn desk. "Someone's trying to kill us."

The deputy frowned and walked to the front door. He locked it and pulled down the shade.

Good. He was taking them seriously.

He slid behind his desk and grabbed his pad and pen. "Give me your names and I'll take your statements."

"I'm Kelsey Chambers."

"Jake Jacobson."

The deputy looked up, surprise clearly written on his face. "You made it."

Huh?

"Someone reported you missing." He swiveled around in his chair to pull something out of the fax machine.

Kelsey's spirits lifted. "Oh, thank goodness. So there's been a search and rescue going on."

"No. Search and recovery."

She shook her head, confused. "Search and recovery?"

Jake squeezed her shoulder. "Who reported us missing?" he asked.

Something in his tone was off.

The deputy stood from behind his desk. He opened the door to the room in the back and gestured for them to enter. Kelsey frowned. She wanted to give her statement. To understand what was going on. But at least someone had tried to get them help.

Kelsey hobbled through the door, Jake at her side. She

sat in the chair next to another desk. Two jail cells were behind that.

The deputy snapped handcuffs on Jake's wrist before either of them had a chance to blink. Jake didn't resist, a defeated expression on his face. His eyes told her that he was sorry he'd let her down.

"No," she said, attempting to stand. "This is all wrong. You've got the wrong person."

"Davis Burroughs reported you missing, along with an item that belongs to him."

"We didn't steal it," she said. "Davis is the thief. He has a smuggling operation going on. We were just caught in the middle and have been trying to get to safety. To tell the police."

Davis is a thief. And potentially a murderer.

Kelsey pressed her face to her hands, feeling dry racking sobs just under the surface. She held them back. Now wasn't the time to lose it. When she glanced back up, the deputy was looking at her. The unwelcome, knowing look in his eyes sent a chill down her spine—he was part of it.

"And search and recovery, little missy, means that everyone thinks you're already dead." The deputy winked.

EIGHTEEN

The deputy pulled his weapon out, apparently concerned that Jake would try something even though he'd been handcuffed.

Then Jake was patted down. Searching for the map? Coming up empty-handed he opened one of the cells. "Inside."

"What about Miranda rights? My phone call?" Jake glowered.

The deputy chuckled.

"You're in on this, too, then." Jake's disappointment was palpable.

They'd made it this far only to come to the wrong person for help. Shoulders down, Jake stepped inside the cell. With a gun pointed at him, there wasn't much more he could do except risk getting shot again.

"What are you going to do with her?" Jake asked.

"She goes in a cell, too." But when the deputy shut the cell behind Jake and locked it, Kelsey's pulse spiked. "After she gives me the map."

He eyed the jackets she wore—Jake's jacket on top of her own. He must presume she was protecting the small slip of paper that some thought worth a life or two.

"I don't have it. We lost it during our ordeal in the woods. And Jake—" she gestured to him as she spoke to the deputy "—has been shot. He needs a doctor."

The deputy frowned and scratched his head. "Take the jacket off and show me there's no map on you."

Kelsey first removed Jake's jacket and the deputy rummaged through the pockets as she removed her own lightweight windbreaker. After he made swift work of the jacket, his gaze moved over her as if he had X-ray vision.

Then he opened the door to the cell next to Jake's. "And you, in here."

"She sprained her ankle," Jake said. "You'll have to help her."

"No," she protested. The last thing she wanted was help from him. Grabbing hold of the cell bars as she maneuvered into her cell, she ignored his smirk.

"Why are you locking us up? We don't have it. We're not involved," she said, but knew her efforts were wasted.

"It's out of my hands now," the deputy said.

The cell door clanked behind her. There wasn't any way they would get out of this.

"Can we at least get some water? Some food?" Jake asked.

"You won't be here long enough." The deputy exited the room to enter the front office. Voices resounded but she couldn't make them out.

Jake moved to stand close to the wall of bars that separated them. "You'd think they could at least put us in the same cell," he said with a grin.

"I'm not in the mood for humor." Kelsey leaned forward, pressing her forehead into her arms.

"Sorry, but I had to try." Jake paced. "Listen, we have to think. To prepare for what's coming. Make an escape plan. They're going to want the map and we don't have it."

"We can't tell them about Eric."

"He's long gone by now, if it comes to that. I wouldn't worry about him."

"Yeah, and once we tell them, we're as good as dead anyway." Kelsey made her way over to the chair resting in the corner next to Jake's cell. "In fact, according to the deputy, we're already assumed dead. No one expects to find us alive."

With that, tears burst out the corners of her eyes. Angry tears. They had fought so hard to make it here and now this?

Your rod and Your staff, they comfort me.

God, where are Your rod and Your staff right now? I don't understand!

Jake's chair scraped the floor as he scooted it next to where she sat. If they fell back to torturing him again, she didn't see how he would make it through this time, no matter how strong he was. At this moment, everything seemed completely hopeless. Kelsey wasn't sure she'd ever experienced what it felt like to be stripped of all hope. Even in the face of everything that had happened before, she'd harbored a sense of optimism, a small light shining somewhere inside her.

But now? A dark abyss had snuffed out that light.

"I wish I wasn't in cuffs, then I could slip my arms through and hold you."

"But the bars would stand between us. We couldn't pretend they weren't there." She drew in a pathetic, ragged breath. "There's always something standing between us, isn't there?"

All the images of that night she'd gone to his apartment to have dinner, full of hope and expectancy, played across her mind once more, and she was helpless to stop them now. She'd let her issues keep her from Jake. A man who through this whole ordeal had remained dependable and trustworthy, constant in his attempts to protect her and get her to safety. And maybe even constant in his love for her—though he hadn't said it in so many words.

And now... "Jake," she whispered, hating the defeated rasp of her trembling voice.

"Don't look at me like that." The gentle reassurances that lit his eyes moments before faded. "I've let you down. Let everyone down. I can't take feeling like I've failed you again." He stood then and scraped his hands through his hair.

Oh, Jake… He felt that way because she'd let him. Because she'd not been willing to tell him how she felt while he was conscious. But that was all she had left now. Her words. She intended to use them this time.

"Everything that tore us apart before seems completely ridiculous right now."

He sighed, but said nothing. Was he going to leave her to do all the talking?

He drew in a long breath, and she tensed, waiting for what would come.

"So now you want to have a heart-to-heart." A statement, not a question. The sudden change in his attitude scared her.

Kelsey squeezed her eyes—his response wasn't what she had expected. Maybe he wasn't interested in exploring a renewed relationship with her should they somehow escape alive.

"I'm impressed, actually, that you're willing to talk now that you know I can hear you."

His words weren't gentle or seasoned with humor, and Kelsey fought the need to clam up again. Putting her feelings out there for him to stomp on wasn't what she wanted. "If you heard me, then you know how I feel. I need to know how *you* feel."

He looked at the ceiling, and she figured he was thinking how pointless it would be now. Then again, maybe now was the only time they had left to lay it all out there.

He pressed his face against the bars near her, but didn't look in her eyes. "That night…I was going to propose."

Kelsey gasped.

The door swung open. A gray-haired woman leaned in, her gaze skirted the room, avoiding the two inmates. "Travis?"

"Help us!" Kelsey and Jake yelled simultaneously.

The woman left, shutting the door again.

"No, please, you have to help us," Kelsey cried. "We've been kidnapped."

Nothing.

The woman had left them to their deputy abductor. Kelsey and Jake shared a look—finally. His eyes found hers and searched, hope and defeat twisted in a terrible knot.

Her mind wrapped around his words, struggling to comprehend them. *Jake had planned to propose?*

The door creaked open again and the woman cautiously entered.

"We need to use your cell phone," Jake said. "I need to call for help. We weren't given our phone call."

"The deputy is involved in a crime," Kelsey pleaded.

The door remained open—showing that the front room was empty—and the woman glanced behind her, worry on her face. "I'm sorry, I can't give you a phone. I don't know what I can do."

"Then make a call for us." Jake's voice was desperate. He rattled off a cell number. "He's my brother. Just tell him where we are. That we're still alive."

The front door swung open and the woman's eyes widened. She turned abruptly to see the deputy. "There you are. Was just looking for you."

She shut the door behind her.

"I told you never…" His angry voice faded after another door shut and it seemed they had exited the office out the front.

What would happen to the woman now? Was she in danger because she'd seen them alive?

Jake sank to the chair close to where Kelsey sat in her own cell. He wished he wasn't in the handcuffs. How long would it be before they were transported elsewhere? He had to get them out of here. He couldn't give up on saving them. On saving her. Even when the situation seemed impossible.

"Yes," she whispered.

"Huh?" he glanced up to see her watching him with her golden hazel eyes.

He never could have imagined this moment. The two of them staring at each other through the bars of a jail cell.

"I would have said yes."

To his proposal? He shook his head and looked away. "It doesn't matter now."

To think—if that moment in time had ended differently, maybe neither one of them would be here, facing an impossible situation. Certain death.

"Because you don't feel the same way?" she asked, probing for an answer.

"I didn't say that, but when I have this…*discussion*…with you, there isn't going to be anything standing in the way." He wanted to hold her and kiss her and know she would trust him, believe him and be committed to him. Admittedly, he'd crossed a metaphorical threshold during this crisis—he'd determined he wouldn't fall in love again, or have anything to do with Kelsey in that way. But she was all he ever wanted, and still wanted. *Needed*…

"Don't you see? We might not get the chance to say everything after this. That's why I want to have the heart-to-heart now."

Maybe she had a point. Maybe they weren't going to get another chance to speak.

"Okay. Here's what I think about us. I need you to trust me. To believe me, even when it doesn't appear like you can. That's what I want in a relationship." Was he asking too much?

He bolted from the chair, wishing he hadn't blurted that out. The words sounded ludicrous now. Would *he* even agree to those terms?

Would he trust Kelsey, believe her, even when it looked like he couldn't?

"What you're asking… I…"

The back door to the jail flew open and the deputy stepped inside. "Time to go."

He shared a glance with Kelsey. They should have talked about escaping instead of their relationship like they were going to have a tomorrow.

Or like they weren't.

"We don't have what you want," Jake said. "Just let us go. We lost it in the woods. You already searched us."

The deputy frowned. "I've got my orders."

Orders from Burroughs? Jake looked at the deputy again, angling to talk some sense into the man. "You realize how much trouble you're in? You have the power to change the outcome here. Don't get murder on your hands, too."

The deputy ushered Kelsey out of the jail cell, leaving Jake behind.

NINETEEN

When the deputy gripped her arm to help her walk, she glanced over her shoulder at Jake and didn't look away until she stepped through the back door into the alley behind the building. An SUV sat idling. She considered trying to kick or fight her way free, but knew she couldn't run. It would be pointless to waste her energy.

The deputy eased her into the seat behind the front passenger seat. Someone was already in the back and Kelsey avoided looking at him.

"Where are you taking me?" Would Jake be brought along, too?

"Buckle up. It's the law, you know," the deputy said.

"Please," she said, hating the whimper in her voice. "Please, help us."

"It's out of my hands."

He shut her in. The door on the opposite side opened and someone shoved Jake into the vehicle to sit next to her. Relief swept through her but she wasn't sure if she was glad to see him or not. He might be safer in the jail cell. She prayed the woman who'd seen them would contact Jake's brother to send them help in time. Kelsey put her hand on Jake's arm, sliding it down and behind his back to feel his still-cuffed wrists. Something pressed at the back of her neck. She stiffened.

"Keep your hands to yourself unless you want the cuffs,

too," the man seated behind her finally spoke up. He just sounded like more of the same to Kelsey. "You make a wrong move and she gets it, understand?"

Jake nodded. "Something happens to her and you can forget about ever finding the map."

Even though I walk through the valley of the shadow of death...

Lord, I'm definitely in the valley here but I do fear evil. Every time we think we're getting somewhere, another bad guy turns up. Please. Help. Us.

She didn't consciously voice it, but in her deepest heart, she knew she didn't trust God to help them. Not anymore. And with that realization, she knew she'd never been in a darker place.

A man she'd never seen before drove the vehicle. She and Jake were in the middle seat, and the guy holding a weapon sat behind them, guarding them. She assumed they were working with Davis, because of what the deputy had said, but how many people were involved in this?

Tension emanated from all angles in the vehicle as it moved through the cloud of fog that grew denser the farther they went. Where on earth were they headed this time? Why didn't they just realize that Kelsey and Jake didn't have the map?

The vehicle turned into the marina.

Great. Another marina. Another boating nightmare. She leaned her head back against the seat rest, aware of the muzzle of the gun still pressed against her skull. But the guy behind her had given her a little room to breathe, at least. Like it mattered. There was no fighting their way out of this with her lame and Jake cuffed.

Jake had wanted to save their heart-to-heart for the right time. Maybe this wasn't the ideal time, but it could be the only chance she had left. And even if she couldn't tell him everything he wanted to hear, there was still something she could say.

"I still love you, Jake."

His gaze jerked over to her. "Not now, Kelsey."

Would saying the words put them in more danger? Doubtful. "Why not? This could be my last chance to tell you." She allowed a soft smile. "You're awake. Coherent. Can understand me. Can respond. I had to tell you that I would have said yes, because I loved you then. And I love you now."

"Women," the voice from the backseat huffed. "Stop the rambling, would you?"

The muzzle of the gun shoved her head forward. Though dread carved lines in Jake's features, he managed a grin. "You have either the worst timing or the best."

She knew what he meant. His words served as a reminder that they were both about to die. Like she needed one with a gun pressed against her head.

The SUV pulled to a stop on the pier and Kelsey caught sight of several boats docked there, but not *The Buccaneer*. The pressure on her head eased as the man behind her lifted his weapon and whacked Jake on the head, knocking him out.

"Jake!" Kelsey's outcry was met with silence from him. She reached over and gripped his head as he leaned to the side, pressing her face into his hair, her tears washing down and disappearing into his thick dark strands, glad now that she'd told him she loved him.

The door on his side of the SUV opened and two men hauled Jake out, tearing him from her grip.

Jake stirred, resting at an awkward angle, and recognized the familiar throb that resulted from being knocked unconscious.

How many times would he have to experience that? Add to that the raw soreness that coursed through him every time he moved his arm or stretched. Carrying Kelsey hadn't aided in his healing. In fact, he was almost sure the gunshot wound had broken open and had bled again. But Eric had done an excellent job of patching him up, so he wouldn't worry too much about that. For now, he needed to get his bearings.

He opened his lids and scanned his room, actually surprised they had left him alive. Surprised they hadn't dumped him in the ocean. The thought sent a chill through him. At the end of this ordeal, that could very well be his fate. Once he thought about it he realized that for now, they wanted to keep him around for insurance because he could lead them to the map.

Jake took in his surroundings—a nice cabin with a double bed. On the luxurious yacht he'd seen as they had approached the marina? He scratched his head.

Whose yacht was this?

Davis Burroughs's? They definitely weren't in Burroughs's care. Had to be someone more powerful. Someone who hadn't gotten behind on their payments. Jake almost laughed.

That's why the map was so important—Burroughs needed the money. And Lennon needed it, too. Jake sat up, and for the first time he noticed the cuffs were gone. He didn't understand. Weren't they afraid he'd attempt to escape again?

That's when he noticed the black tuxedo displayed on a hook rather than tucked away in the closet, as if he was supposed to see it. Maybe even put it on. Nah, he wasn't thinking clearly.

They'd tossed his limp body in someone else's room. But whose?

On the small table in the corner, a steak and baked potato filled out a plate with full settings—knife included.

Huh?

What's going on? A pang shot through Jake's stomach. He approached the table and held his palm over the food. Cold. He stuck the knife in his pocket.

Someone had made a big mistake, leaving a knife for him. Or had they?

Jake tried the door. Locked from the outside. Right. None

of this made any sense. He pounded on the door, which opened promptly to reveal a husky man dressed in a tux. His partner remained in position next to the door.

Jake fingered the knife in his pocket and considered trying to attack, but if he was going to succeed this time, he needed more information and a plan.

The man grunted—his way of asking what Jake wanted.

"Oh, thanks, buddy. I locked myself in." Jake tried to squeeze by. Might as well go for broke.

A wry grin appeared on the beefy guy's face. "You can't leave until you're wearing the tux."

Jake blinked. Now that was a new one. That had to be the last thing he ever expected to hear. Not, *Get back in your room if you want to live.* Or a fist in the gut like he would have expected. This was a much different crew than had been charged with his handling in the past. Much different and with the hint of a Russian accent.

Regardless, Jake hadn't seriously thought he'd be allowed to leave. "So what am I? A prisoner? Or a guest?"

The guy's nose crinkled. "You smell like something from the gutter. You might try the shower. And then ask me."

While a hot shower and dinner sounded like a dream come true, Jake wasn't buying it. "What's this all about, big guy? And where's my lady friend?"

"She'll be at the party. But you're not going until you're in the tux, smelling like a rose."

Jake snorted. This was crazy. But he'd play along.

"Okay, well, I'm going to shower and there'd better be a plate of hot, fresh food on that table when I'm done. The one in there has gone cold. I like my rib eye medium well."

Yeah. Might as well go for broke.

She'll be at the party.

He'd hold on to that for now.

TWENTY

Kelsey rubbed her arms and took in the luxurious room. It was bigger than any she'd seen in her brief experience with boating. Maybe she'd seen one in a movie or a show about the rich and famous, but never in person.

She and Jake had spent the past several hours on a boat that had transported them to a city harbor and a much bigger yacht. Jake, of course, wouldn't know where he was when and if he woke up. Grief pooled in her stomach at the unfairness of it all. She moved to the door. It might be locked from the outside, but she had to check. She slammed it with her fist. *Jake...*

What had they done with him? Pain stabbed through her hand. Why had God created women so much weaker than men? She wanted to slide to the floor and cry. Why hadn't she told him she could trust him? That's all he'd wanted to hear from her.

Was it really so hard?

Kelsey sank to the crimson-silk-covered bed with one question on her mind—was Jake trustworthy? As she pondered it, realization dawned. She pressed her face into her hands as she was overcome by a wash of shame. *Kelsey* was the one who couldn't be trusted. Jake couldn't count on her to stick around.

She had to change that. Somehow.

A soft knock on the door startled her. Jake? She limped forward, expecting, hoping to see Jake walk through, and doubting it at the same time. The door eased open.

A man dressed in a tuxedo stepped into the room, his rich cologne wrapping around her.

Davis.

With everything in her, she wanted to rail at him, but the words caught in her throat.

He shut the door behind him. "I'm so sorry that you got caught in the middle of this."

"How can you pretend to be sorry?" she asked. "What did you think would happen when you hired me to be a cover for your pathetic smuggling operation?" With that she found the nerve to step forward and swing her palm, full force toward his face—

He caught her wrist in midair. Fury boiled inside. How she would have loved to make contact. She ripped her arm from his grip.

He shook his head, regret twisting across his features. "You have it all wrong. I never meant for any of this to happen. For you to be involved."

"How could I not be involved when I was on *The Buccaneer?* The vessel you used in your smuggling operation?"

A nervous laugh escaped, cracking through his frown. Kelsey moved away from him, but didn't turn her back.

"Please, allow me to explain," he said.

She crossed her arms.

"From the articles you sent me so far, I think you're an excellent travel writer. So, I guess this means I'll be losing you?" Another nervous laugh.

A scoff worked its way up her throat. Didn't he realize he was going to jail? "And you're a criminal, stealing and smuggling antiquities. Kidnapping and murder charges will put you away for a long time. I don't think you're going to be around for me to work for."

Davis held up his palms in surrender. "Whoa. I'm not really sure what you're talking about. I'm not a criminal, Kelsey. I'm a little wounded that you so readily believe that."

"How can you think you're not committing crimes?"

"I return important relics—stolen relics, I might add—to their rightful owners, that's all."

Just returning it to its rightful owner. Jake's words from days ago rippled through her thoughts. So the two men weren't that different after all. Kelsey looked away. Was *she* different, either? She'd taken the map, planning to return it, as well.

Confusion washed over her. "I'm here on this boat because I was abducted, kidnapped by someone working for you."

"I'm sorry if you were hurt. I simply needed you here so I could explain. Neely tried to double-cross me, and admittedly, I made a mistake. I thought I could trust him. I pride myself in being a good judge of character." He closed in on her. "You were supposed to be done with your assignment and far away from *The Buccaneer* before any delivery was made."

Kelsey recalled that she'd agreed to stay an extra day so Neely and his wife could stay on the island for their anniversary. Then it hit her—did Davis even know about Lennon?

"I'm not sure Neely double-crossed you," she said. "*The Buccaneer* was hijacked and I was abducted along with a friend of mine by Lennon and his men. From what I gathered, Lennon hates you. And he said that Neely was dead." She sank into a plush chair, exhaustion moving over her like a thick fog.

A soft frown edged into his brows. "I don't understand. Neely...dead? And who is Lennon?"

Indeed. "The guy who kidnapped me. He wants the map, too, and he asked a lot of questions about you. I don't know his real name, it's just that he wears these round John Lennon glasses and I started to think of him as Lennon."

Davis's face reddened. "Jonathan Hunter." He ground out the name.

"Oh, so you know him. He didn't seem to know all that much about you, considering all his questions."

"I guess you could say he's an archrival."

Kelsey gave a mock nod. "I see. He collects books and antiquities, too. Gathers them to return them to their *rightful* owners. Kills people who get in his way."

Another nervous laugh escaped. "He *does* return items, but usually for a price. He wants the compensation this time. Just like I do. But I promise, I'd never kill anyone to get it." He rubbed his temples, clearly disturbed by the news.

No, you'd just kidnap them when it suits you.

"I think Lennon, I mean Hunter, and his men tried to beat information out of Captain Neely. Killing him wasn't their intent, though it didn't seem to upset them. Then they tried to get it out of me and Jake, but I knew nothing about what you'd smuggled. I've spent the last several days running for my life only to be whisked away to this yacht by a sheriff's deputy acting on your behalf." Kelsey huffed. "I mean it, Davis, what is going on?"

"I reported you missing to a few of my contacts. I…uh… When I received the call that you'd been found, I asked that you be delivered here tonight, so I might make amends. So I could explain things."

Why hadn't he reported her missing to the authorities, the *real* authorities, instead? "Delivered here tonight. Do you hear yourself? I was abducted, brought here against my will."

He'd known something was awry when Neely didn't turn up and both *The Buccaneer* and Kelsey were missing, so he'd panicked and tried to cover his own rear first. And she was pretty sure his real reasons for bringing her to the boat had nothing to do with "making amends" at all.

She shook her head. "I don't hear anything about the map in there. Don't try to tell me that isn't part of why I'm here. I'm guessing the *rightful owner* also owns this yacht and you were supposed to deliver the map to him. But since you can't, you're delivering me. You should know, too, that Lennon—or Hunter as you call him—and his men followed me and my friend into the wilderness." She paused. That was another long story. "They knew we were headed to Hood. My point is I'm not so sure he's given up yet."

Davis's expression grew somber and a vein in his temple pulsed. "This changes everything. Kelsey, listen to me. We're both in a lot of trouble."

The man had some nerve. "Both? *I'm* not the one in trouble. *You* are. And what about Jake?"

"Ah, the man who came with you."

"Yes. Jake is…a friend." No point in making this more convoluted by mentioning Jake's attempt to repossess Davis's boat. Or stating that Jake was much more than a friend.

Davis nodded. "I see. Well, you need to change into the dress."

He gestured to the wall at the far end of the room where a silky lavender evening gown hung.

"Are you insane? I'm not changing into a dress for you!"

"You will if you want to live. Like you've already figured out, this yacht doesn't belong to me. In fact, it's one of the largest private yachts in the world. It belongs to the man who wants the map. A powerful, dangerous man."

Davis swallowed, the sound loud enough for Kelsey to hear. "I've already taken a chunk of his money to guarantee delivery. Money I can't return." He frowned, looking distracted by his thoughts. "Not sure what Hunter thinks he'll gain by smuggling it right from under my nose. There's just no honor."

"No honor among thieves, that is." Kelsey enjoyed driving those words into Davis's heart. "Besides, what does any of it have to do with me or Jake? We don't have the stupid map."

"If all I can do is deliver you with the information, that's what I have to do. Even if it's just to say you don't have the map because Jonathan Hunter took it." Moisture beaded his forehead. "That way, maybe we can all walk away from this. And I stress, *maybe*."

The fear in his eyes rocked her—he didn't care that he didn't have the map, only that he delivered something tonight. And that something was Kelsey because she'd been on *The Buccaneer*. What a coward he was, throwing her to this man in his place.

Would she be able to keep her word to Eric? Would she be made to choose between her life and her promise? To give him away? Could she persuade Jake to keep it to himself no matter what?

"Tell me something, Davis. Why me?"

"I'm not sure I understand."

"Was running into me just an accident? Or did you handpick me, after our chance run-in? Did you pursue a friendship with me so you could eventually hire me because I would be too naive to figure out your cover?"

"You weren't supposed to be involved with this at all," he said. "You were only finishing out an assignment on the yacht, remember? Our meeting wasn't something I planned. I…I was an idiot to put you in that situation. But as I've already explained, I didn't plan for any of this to happen."

"No one ever does." Kelsey stared at the dress.

"I admit, I've never dealt with such a high-dollar item, or such a high-profile collector, but my finances got out of control, took a nosedive. This opportunity seemed like the answer. If everything had gone as planned, it would have *been* the answer. And it could still work, if we play everything right."

Without the map, it wouldn't work. Why couldn't Davis see that? And even if the collector let her go, did he think she would just walk away without reporting her story to the police?

Davis searched her eyes. "Haven't you ever made a mistake, Kelsey?"

Apparently he was counting on mercy. On her to keep quiet out of some sense of perverted loyalty. Jake's face ripped across her mind from when she'd broken things off with him. Hurt pouring from his eyes. She squeezed hers shut now, hating the images of that moment.

"Yes…I have. But nothing like this. Nothing that affected others…" Well, maybe that wasn't quite true, but at least she hadn't caused harm in such a devastating way.

"I need you to understand how important it is for you to cooperate. We need to deliver tonight and big or we could all lose our lives. So you should get into that dress, for starters."

"Why do I have to get dressed up to meet this guy? I can simply tell you what I know, which isn't much, and you can deliver the information. You can let me and Jake go." Now Kelsey was the one to plead. "Please, Davis, if you mean what you said, that you never meant for any of this to happen, then you have to get us out of here. Don't leave us at the mercy of this man who apparently values something old and dead more than the living."

"I'm two steps ahead of you. There's a party on the boat tonight. You'll blend in wearing that dress."

Kelsey shrugged. "What's going to keep me from telling someone at the party I've been kidnapped? From calling the police with someone's cell phone? Or leaving the party?" What a complete fool she was to bring any of that up.

Davis gave her a confused look. "Are you serious? These people are Ivanov's people."

"Ivanov?" *Was he some sort of Russian mob leader? Oh, Davis, what have you done?*

"The guests are at his party on his yacht. Are you really going to try to convince one of them that you've been kidnapped when you don't have a clue who you can trust?"

"I might." Kelsey enjoyed the smirk she gave Davis.

"Do that at great risk to your life. My life. And your friend's life. Ivanov owns every person on this boat."

Including you, Davis. "And what about Jake? You never answered me before."

"I promise you, I'll do everything I can to remove you and your friend from harm's way as soon as I can. Just play along a little longer. I've already made arrangements for the both of you to be at the party."

"I don't think he'll be that willing to jump through your hoops."

"He will if he wants to see you. In fact, he's already jumping."

Jake shrugged into the suit jacket. Did he really want to go through with this? He felt like a baboon in this suit but at least he didn't smell like one anymore.

She'll be at the party.

He kept his thoughts focused on one thing—get to that party. Get to Kelsey. And get out.

He'd scarfed down the original plate of steak and baked potato, though it was cold, to give him much-needed sustenance. He'd have to speak to the guy running this show about the poor service. The thought almost brought a chuckle.

That is, when he saw the man responsible for what had happened to them. And he hoped he might get the chance to see the guy—whoever he was—during his and Kelsey's great escape.

Their great escape. He'd done such a brilliant job so far.

Head, guts, heart.

His head and his guts hadn't done much for them, but now, he was nearing the end of this particular race and to make it through, to be a winner, he'd have to run the rest with his heart.

He'd have to draw on that place inside that allowed people to rise above themselves. To accomplish the impossible.

And to that end, he would put on the tux and give the *appearance* of cooperating. He examined himself in the mirror and fixed the bow tie, cringing inside. He ran his hand down his smooth chin, compliments of the razor in the shower. He was feeling like his old self again. That is, if he ignored the dull throbbing in his arm and head…and the dull throbbing in his heart.

He never thought he'd see himself in a tux again after his brother's wedding, except for his own wedding day. Regret swirled in his gut. Why couldn't he and Kelsey have gotten married? They wouldn't be on this yacht today, facing unknown dangers, facing death.

Jake stared into his own eyes. How many times would she tell him she loved him without hearing the words from him in return? He'd thought them, but he'd feared saying them.

He'd hoped to tell her at the right moment but now he wasn't sure if that moment would ever come. Loving Kelsey Chambers, telling her that he loved her, was a gigantic risk to his heart. She could take off again. Leave him hanging. She'd done it before.

In the past, she'd been unwilling to trust. Unwilling to forgive. But now Jake faced a big decision—loving her anyway, in spite of what he saw as a big flaw in her character. And he saw too clearly now that he'd not been willing to fully sacrifice either his heart or his life—the way a man should.

Squeezing the counter, his knuckles white, Jake sucked in a few breaths, composing his thoughts. First, he had to go to a party. With people. People would have cell phones. They could be informed of the situation.

What was the guy in charge thinking? It was kind of like leaving the knife—maybe the person in charge *wasn't* thinking, after all. Maybe the person in charge was being careless. But nothing about this operation appeared careless.

Except Jake. He was careless. Deep inside he knew that he'd failed miserably through this experience. Failed to save Kelsey when the opportunities had been there.

Why, God? Why am I such a complete joke? Why did I drift

*away from You? I need You now, I know that. And I know
that when I'm weak, You're strong. So please see my weakness, take this joke of a hero and be strong for me. Help me
to save Kelsey, to get us out of this.*

Jake straightened the tux, took another breath, lifted his
fist and knocked on the door.

His beefy guard opened it and gave half a grin. "Much
better."

Funny how those words echoed Jake's thoughts exactly.

"Where's the party?" He was ready to see Kelsey.

"First, a few rules that I'm sure you'll appreciate. No one
goes anywhere on this rig without an escort."

Figured. "And you're my escort?"

The guy shook his head with his thick neck. "I'm half of
your escort. For you, there are two of us."

The other guard turned to face Jake but didn't grin.

The great escape. Right.

TWENTY-ONE

Kelsey slid her hands up the zipper in the back and struggled.

No way would she ask someone for help. And who thought she could wear a size six anyway? She sucked in her breath and pulled on the zipper.

One.

More.

Time.

There. Now, she'd have to be careful not to breathe, eat or laugh, and she might actually make it through this night. The dress itself didn't look too tight on her, but the waist cinched at just the absolute worst place. And the shoes. How was she expected to wear these gorgeous high heels with a sprained ankle?

But what was she thinking? She had no plans to eat or laugh. The tight dress was a trivial matter in light of her abduction. The shoes even less important. Staring in the mirror, she exhaled, sending a stray curl fluttering. Sliding her hand down the front so she could feel the stunning silky fabric, she held in her stomach and considered her appearance. How sad that she was getting all dressed up for this…this… what was it anyway?

She felt like that old cliché about a lamb being led to the slaughter.

All she could think was she'd come to this moment in time because of a single decision. A different decision, and she'd be somewhere else right now. She and Jake both. A person wasn't supposed to think of life in those terms. Who could manage their life if they agonized over every choice along the way?

I could have trusted him.

Right now, I'd be somewhere else. With him. I could have been Mrs. Jake Jacobson.

Even if she and Jake were allowed to walk away tonight and live to pursue their dreams, she had a feeling that Jake wasn't about to give her a second chance. Funny, that. She would think it would be the other way around—him wanting the second chance with her to make up for his mistakes. But it wasn't like that at all. And funny, too, that his spiel about mercy trumping judgment didn't count when it came to her—he hadn't forgiven her for not believing him.

But why pick on him? She had her own problems. How could she trust Jake when she couldn't even trust God? Here she was going to a room filled with people, and she didn't get the sense she'd be able to escape even then.

"God, I want to trust You, but the situation seems impossible, even for You," she whispered. *Even for You.*

You prepare a table before me in the presence of my enemies. The verse from Psalm 23 echoed through her heart.

She was going to a party where her enemies would definitely be present. Closing her eyes, she forced her heart and mind to let go, just a little. She needed to trust that God would see her through.

"Okay, God, I'm going to believe in You, trust You completely." Easy enough to say, but harder to do. And what about trusting Jake?

As she pondered all these issues, Kelsey used the makeup kit she'd found in the drawer in a futile attempt to hide the circles under her eyes. Anyone could take one look at her, even in this dress, and know something was wrong.

She glanced at the door, wondering if Davis would come to get her. She'd assumed she was supposed to wait for him. What would the next fifteen minutes, thirty…the next hour bring? Her hands trembled at the thought and with that, she was done waiting on Davis. Dangling the strap of the heels on her finger, she moved to the door and wrapped her palm around the knob, expecting it to be locked.

You prepare a table for me…

Kelsey twisted the knob and to her surprise the door opened. A man wearing a tux stood guard. Was he armed?

She looked past him down the hall both ways. Where was Davis? "How do I get to the party?"

"Right this way." He gestured for her to walk ahead of him.

She decided to leave the shoes and tossed them back into the room. She shut the door behind her.

Though her ankle had improved somewhat, pain shot up her leg as she walked. She worked to ignore the pulsating throb, doing her best to move steadily in her bare feet. At least the dress hid her feet unless someone looked closely. But no way could she get on those heels, much less walk in them. "Allow me," her guard said and offered his elbow. She noticed he had the hint of a Russian accent. "I can help you walk."

She gave him a soft smile, wondering how much he knew about her predicament. By the look in his eyes, she guessed he wasn't allowed to let her out of his sight.

He ushered her slowly down a hallway. Kelsey tried to calm herself, repeating the Bible verse.

"Psalm 23," the guard said.

"Pardon?" She lifted her eyes to him.

"My mother," he said. "That was her favorite."

Kelsey hadn't realized she'd said the verses out loud, but before she could respond, they rounded the corner where more men in tuxedos stood outside double doors. Were they guards or guests? Once inside the opulent room filled with elegant people, Kelsey released the guard's arm.

He leaned in to whisper. "No one leaves the room without an escort."

Kelsey frowned and searched the room for Jake. Davis had assured her that Jake would be here. Sidling up to a woman drinking punch at a food-adorned table, Kelsey leaned against the table, getting some weight off her ankle.

"Are you all right?" the woman asked.

"No, actually." Kelsey kept her voice low, glancing around to make sure no one paid her unwanted attention.

How did she tell this woman she'd been kidnapped? The woman seemed mildly annoyed with Kelsey rather than truly concerned. Trusting her with Kelsey's predicament suddenly didn't seem like a good idea just as Davis had warned. Still, she could hardly sink much deeper into the mire. "Listen, I'm being held here against my will. Can I borrow your cell? I need to call for help."

The woman laughed. "You're good."

Kelsey frowned. Her words sounded ridiculous even to her own ears. "Seriously, I lost my cell, can I borrow yours? I have an emergency."

"We had to leave our cells at the door, remember?" The woman gave her a curious look.

Unbelievable. "Who would actually give up their cell phone?"

"Who wouldn't if it meant a chance to attend a Roman Ivanov party on his luxury yacht?" The woman studied Kelsey and leaned closer. "I don't know if you've met him or you're someone's date for tonight, but you need to act like you're enjoying yourself."

Kelsey realized there was no way to convince this woman she'd really been kidnapped. Considering Davis's warnings, she smiled and moved away from the woman. Blend in and escape. Drawing this Ivanov's attention wasn't a good idea before she was forced into his presence. She hoped to be gone before that happened.

Then she spotted Jake across the room. Wearing a tux. He was like…a knight come to save her.

Her breath caught. Tears burned at the back of her eyes.

The ordeal they'd been through together somehow faded—though never too far—when her eyes locked with Jake's and she smiled, infused with relief and hope she'd not felt for a long time. Deep down, she knew that…

She could trust again.

In her peripheral vision, she didn't miss the moment when Davis stepped into the room, followed by another, formidable-looking man who seemed to draw attention from the guests.

Roman Ivanov.

The most beautiful woman in the world.

The woman who would have been his bride. Jake couldn't imagine her looking any more beautiful on her wedding day. Even though he could tell she was exhausted. Scared. But there was definitely a glow about her tonight. A light he hadn't seen before.

Who had selected that dress for her? The guy had known what he was doing when he'd picked it out. He'd known Kelsey.

Had to have been Burroughs.

Acid swirled hot in Jake's gut. He couldn't wait to get his hands on the man responsible for putting their lives in jeopardy. He worked his way through the crowd toward Kelsey. He'd already tried his hand at getting help, but that hadn't worked very well considering the first person he talked to was cousin to the yacht owner. Jake had known to say nothing to anyone in this room after that.

His two guards weren't too far behind, having been instructed he was a flight risk. But so far Jake hadn't been much of a threat to anyone.

That was all about to change, and he had no plans to leave without Kelsey. He needed to make it to her before Burroughs and the party's host—this Ivanov character that everyone kept talking about—found her. And the two men heading her way, the same as Jake, must be Davis and their *host*.

Someone grabbed his arm. He snapped around to find a beautiful blonde smiling at him. Somehow she wrapped herself in his arms without any effort before he could protest.

"Hey, what are you doing?" Jake tried to step away without drawing attention.

One glance over at Kelsey and he caught the hurt playing on her features, even from across the room. This image was an all-too-familiar reminder of their past. The past he'd desperately tried to leave behind.

"You're just the guy I was looking for," the woman said. Like Jake's guards, he detected a hidden but sophisticated Russian accent.

Jake scowled. "Please, let go. I'm here with someone."

She puckered her lips in a pout as he disentangled himself to make his way to Kelsey, but when he looked up she was gone. When he caught sight of her again, she was chatting it up with Burroughs and the man he'd bet was Ivanov just by the way people reacted to him. He had an air about him that said he owned the place. Owned the people.

Jake hung back, watching. Though Kelsey smiled, there was no doubt she was tense, putting on a show for Burroughs. But why? What had he told her to make her act like she was here willingly?

The threat of facing off with a powerful and dangerous Russian, maybe even related to the Russian mob in some way, had to be enough to make anyone comply. Jake wondered how he would respond when it was his turn.

When I am weak, You are strong.

The next thing he knew, Ivanov was guiding Kelsey through the crowd along with Burroughs.

Not without me, you don't.

He shoved between two men he couldn't get around. Muscular, like bouncers. Probably more of the guards. How many of these goons did Ivanov have on this rig anyway?

Pressing past the men, he was rewarded with questioning scowls, but he didn't have time to worry about them. He had to reach Kelsey before she was carted away to who-knew-where.

Then someone caught Ivanov's attention and after a brief conversation, his expression turned serious. Jake was almost there. Almost to Kelsey.

The man excused himself, again acting as though Kelsey were his guest. Her smile quickly washed away when the man turned his back, and she glared at Burroughs. He frowned, his gaze following Ivanov's. Then he whispered something in Kelsey's ear and left her alone.

Her gaze traveled the room until it landed on Jake.

The initial smile he'd seen on her face when she'd locked eyes with him only moments before was long gone. Wariness had replaced it.

Jake ploughed his way through the throng, wondering at the maximum occupancy in this room. "Kelsey," he said and lightly touched her arm.

The warning in her eyes kept him at a distance. Physically and emotionally.

"What was that all about?" He lifted his chin toward the exit Burroughs had left through.

She gave a slight shake of her head. "I don't know. I… He told me that I needed to play my part tonight if I wanted to live. All I could think about was you. If I failed, you'd end up hurt again."

She managed a smile and brushed at the corner of her lids. Her gaze traveled down his torso. "You really know how to take a girl's breath away."

That knot in his throat again. "I've struggled to breathe ever since I saw you in that dress."

A laugh escaped. "You and me both. Whoever thought I could fit into this was crazy."

"No, no they weren't. You're stunning."

Then she looked at him, her eyes warming to his admiration. Whoever said that flattery would get you nowhere?

"Oh, Jake." She glanced around the room.

When she looked back at him, he couldn't stand it any longer. He caught Kelsey up in his arms.

She exhaled—a surprised gasp mixed with relief—and a soft smile spread across her perfect lips.

He urged his focus from her mouth to her eyes. "I thought I'd never make it over to you."

Hurt flitted across her features, threatening to remove her smile. He knew she was thinking about the woman who'd accosted him. But he couldn't do anything about that, just like he couldn't before. Kelsey was just going to have to trust him.

"I'm glad you did," she said.

She pressed her face against his chest and he held her to him, wishing he'd never have to let her go again. He ran his hand down her back, reassuring her, though he felt no certainty himself.

"What are we going to do?" she asked.

With Kelsey in his arms, Jake wanted to stay in the room with these people for the rest of the evening. Maybe he could pretend, and he and Kelsey could leave with the crowd like they were guests all along.

But that wasn't the way of things.

"I'll tell you what we're going to do," he said. "We're going to leave this party."

He let her go and took her hand, tugging her through the crowd.

"No." She stood her ground. "We can't. Not yet."

He paused, turning to hear what she had to say.

"Davis said if we just play along and we tell Ivanov what we know about where the map is, then we'll be free to go. He'll do everything he can to make sure we're out of harm's way."

Incredulity washed through him. "And you believe him?"

Kelsey hesitated. "I don't know what to believe, but it sounds like our only option. You have to admit we haven't exactly gotten anywhere with our attempts to escape. Maybe Davis's plan will work."

Jake chafed at the challenge in her tone. No, Burroughs's plan was not going to work—not except to save anyone but him. "Look, Burroughs is not your friend, Kelsey. He only cares about himself."

"I know it seems that way—"

"*Seems* that way?" Noticing he'd drawn attention, Jake lowered his voice. "Kelsey, it *is* that way. He wants you to cooperate to save his own skin. Otherwise, you'd be somewhere safe instead of here on this yacht, waiting for the firing squad."

Her face grew pale.

Idiot. He shouldn't have said it like that. "Burroughs is the reason you…we…are in this predicament. He is the reason you are here now. You cannot trust him." Jake held his palm out. "But will you trust me?"

TWENTY-TWO

She wanted to trust him. But then Kelsey had watched that woman entangle herself in his arms across the room, and the memories had swept over her. Why did this keep happening to them? Coming between them?

She just wanted this to be over. Jake was right about Davis. What was Davis playing at anyway? She couldn't imagine Ivanov being pleased to know that she'd had the map but lost it in the woods. That simply revealed how terrified Davis was. He'd rather deliver her to Ivanov than nothing. What would a man like Ivanov do with her over the map he wanted? A map she'd lost?

Jake cleared his throat. He stood there palm out, waiting for her answer. She sensed that her response held meaning much bigger than this situation. But she needed something from him, too.

"I trust you as much as you trust me." With the loud conversations and music around them, she hoped he missed the shakiness in her voice.

Brows twisting together, his hopeful look faltered. That told her everything. It told her more than he'd wanted her to know, she was sure. And that hope she'd felt moments before was quickly beginning to fade.

"Let's leave our personal lives, our relationship, out of this one," he said. "Do you trust me with your life?"

She didn't even have to think about it. "Without a doubt."

"Good. Because that's all I really wanted to know." Half of a wry grin slipped into his cheek, and she knew that wasn't the full truth.

He thrust out his hand again like they were good to go, but Kelsey wasn't ready.

"Not so fast."

"What now?" His jaw started working, letting her know he was growing impatient.

"We need to think this through. Talk about it. Maybe you should trust *me* with a plan this time."

He stared at her and blinked, as though that thought had never occurred to him. "Sure. Of course. I just thought since you asked me what we're going to do, you didn't know. But let's hear it. What have you got?"

She nearly laughed at his response. "I know you want to be a hero, Jake. But you don't have to. We can work together. You know a little something about boats. And I know a little something about men."

He raised a brow. "Really."

"Yes. Really. The guy who was guarding my door and escorted me here, he's got a heart. Was a little soft. Maybe I could smile at him or something, catch him off guard. You can disable him somehow then we can escape."

Jake grinned and that grin from him while he was in a tux made her heart jump.

"Although I can see how you could catch a guy off guard, that plan sounds too risky for my tastes. I wouldn't walk into something like that willingly. Also, I don't want you to have to bat your eyelashes at the guards. I'd rather be the one to take the risks."

Murmurs grew in the crowd and Kelsey looked at the door along with Jake. In came Ivanov.

"Time for talk is up." He grabbed her hand and headed for the exit at the opposite side of the room.

They weren't going to get through the guards. What was he thinking? Jake started through the exit, Kelsey in tow, like the guards didn't exist.

A hand pressed against his chest, and he winced, but stopped suddenly, and Kelsey nearly fell. Jake caught her in his arms. She was more worried about the pain he must feel with that beefy hand against his chest wound.

"Where do you think you're going?"

"We need some fresh air."

"Not without an escort, you don't."

"Yeah. I've heard that. So, are you escorting us then?"

The guy scrunched his face and looked across the room as though Ivanov would send him an answer. But the host of the party was surrounded with people admiring him, women fawning over him.

"I don't think you're supposed to leave."

Kelsey lifted her swollen ankle. "I hurt my ankle and I need to sit down. Put some ice on it. You could take us where I can do that. This place is big enough, maybe you have a doctor on board."

Unconvinced, he shook his head. "No one leaves the party."

"Without an escort. Those were the rules. You can go with us," Jake said.

"What's this?" Kelsey's guard appeared.

She leaned heavy against Jake. "My ankle is killing me. I don't want to disturb the party. Just take us some place where I can sit down and put some ice on it." She smiled at him, and saw the warmth cut through his cold veneer.

"This one's mine. I'll take full responsibility," he said.

"Thanks," Kelsey said, flashing a bigger smile at him to seal the deal.

Jake exited the party with her on his arm.

"Hold on. I said you, not him," the man said.

"Please? He's my date for the party. I don't want to go without him."

"I thought Burroughs was her date?" one of the guards said.

"Willis, you're coming, too," her guard said. "You get to watch the guy."

Kelsey shared a knowing look with Jake. She'd gotten to use her idea and it had worked. So far. She hoped her plan wouldn't backfire.

Jake didn't like this. Sure, he'd somehow managed to lose the two guards who'd escorted him from his room. Still, this wasn't what he'd had in mind. He'd planned to insist on some fresh air above deck. He considered setting off the fire alarm, but a panic would ensue and people could get hurt.

He'd seen a few of the guests come and go—with escorts—but not many. There probably weren't enough guards to escort every person individually.

Above deck, Jake might be able to pinpoint exactly where they were. How far from the dock the yacht was anchored. With this many people, they had to be near a populated area.

A jump overboard and a quick swim to shore could mean escape this time. But, no, they were headed somewhere else. Thanks to Kelsey. Somewhere they couldn't use to get off this boat.

Should he try to take down the two guards now and urge Kelsey to make a run for it? "Where are we headed?"

Before the guard answered, Burroughs and Ivanov stepped into the hall, flanked by more of his goons.

Great. This got better by the second.

Burroughs sent Jake a stabbing glare that Jake was only too happy to return. Ivanov offered a smile to Kelsey, but Jake didn't miss the menace behind it. He didn't understand why all the attention fell to her when he was the one who could take them to the map. This was all Burroughs's doing.

"Ah, Miss Chambers." Ivanov lifted his arm, expecting her to grab on. "Just the woman I was looking for."

"Sorry, boss," her guard said. "Her ankle was hurting. We were escorting them to get some ice."

"Well, now you can escort them to my office suite. Get someone to fetch some ice. See if you can find the medic." To Kelsey he said, "I'm so sorry that your medical needs haven't been attended to." If he was Russian, Jake couldn't tell by his accent. His English was perfect.

Kelsey's chest rose and fell with her panic. She tried to smile, but Jake knew her well enough to see her distaste bubbling at the edges. Jake could see Burroughs's displeasure spreading across his features, too. He really was trying to pull something off here. Did Ivanov realize they'd been kidnapped and held against their will? What was really going on here? They were here with nothing to show for it and that made no sense.

"You know, really, I'd prefer just to go home."

Good girl. She was going for broke.

The man angled his head in question.

"You act as if I'm a guest," she said. "But we all know I'm not."

Ivanov's smile instantly fell. "Let's have this discussion elsewhere."

Without another word he nodded at the guards whose demeanors changed, as well. Jake was determined to get out of this without getting hit in the head again. He caught a sideways glimpse of Kelsey's guard. The man looked worried. Maybe she was right—he was a softy or at least was a little soft on Kelsey. Jake understood that feeling.

If it came down to it, and he hoped it wouldn't, which side would this guy fall on?

Kelsey took a step and her ankle failed. Her guard caught her. "Here, let me carry you."

"No," Jake said. "I'll do it."

"No need to fight over me, boys," Kelsey said. "I can walk."

Limp would have been a better term, but she didn't have to go far.

They shoved through the double doors of the man's suite, which included an expansive office space and executive desk. Jake strolled into the room, accompanied by four guards now, and assisted Kelsey into a plush antique chair. Then the guards ushered him to stand next to the wall.

The room was decorated with framed and matted old maps and other antiquities. A glass shelf displayed books that appeared aged, as well. He and Kelsey both gazed around the room wide-eyed.

So this was it. This was what it was all about. Everything they'd been through was over some old piece of paper this powerful man wanted to add to his collection. It was about those who were willing to kidnap or kill in order to put it in his hands for the right price.

And people had battled over doing just that. Whatever had happened to Lennon, Jake wondered. Had he found Eric in the woods? Would Lennon make an appearance, a sudden last attempt to deliver? Or had he given up altogether?

Ivanov entered the room after them and made his way to sit behind the desk. "Now, what's this about not being my guest, Miss Chambers?"

"Are you saying that I'm free to leave when I please? That you didn't know I was kidnapped and brought here?"

He put a finger to his lips and considered her words. He glanced at Burroughs. "That's a very serious accusation that I'll let you take up with Mr. Burroughs after we've concluded our business." He glanced at Burroughs, but then back to

Kelsey. "I was led to believe that you had some information for me."

Was this guy serious? Or just playing innocent to dodge criminal charges?

Burroughs cleared his throat. "I invited Kelsey. I'm sorry if she thought she wasn't a guest. My fault. Kelsey, care to share what you know?"

"Leave us," the man said.

The guards headed for the door.

"I mean all of you. Everyone except Miss Chambers."

Jake didn't budge. "No, I'm with her."

The man pursed his lips.

"No," she said. "He's just a guy I met at the party. Send him back."

"Wait." Burroughs stepped forward. "They came together. He can't go back to the party."

Ivanov frowned and flicked his hand at the guards like they should read his mind. The guards grabbed Jake's arms and started hauling him out the door. Jake wasn't about to go willingly but Kelsey slid a subtle glance his way and in that moment…Jake realized what Kelsey had done for him.

She was the one with the plan, after all.

She'd bought him freedom.

The freedom he would need to save her, and in that moment, he knew she trusted him completely.

TWENTY-THREE

The door shut behind him, sealing Kelsey in the room with a powerful and dangerous man. Jake shrugged off the two goons who'd escorted him into the hallway and took a moment to assess the situation.

He smirked at Burroughs who'd been sent away, too—he wasn't any better off than Jake at the moment. Jake would use that to the fullest.

Burroughs quickly replaced his concerned expression with a smug grin. Jake saw right through him. He was worried. Really worried. Jake might even say Burroughs was afraid for his life because he couldn't control Kelsey or what she said behind those doors.

Now was Jake's chance.

The moment he'd been dreaming of for days now. He lunged at the man and wrapped his fingers around his throat, wanting to strike more fear in him. This man who'd done this to Kelsey. To them.

The guards didn't even try to stop Jake, or maybe his rage had them running scared. Who were they working for anyway? Maybe they wanted to see who was really in charge, and the winner took all.

Jake didn't care. He only saw Burroughs's red face under his rage-filled grip.

He tightened that grip on the man's thick neck. He wouldn't

choke him to death, but God help him, part of him wanted to. Seeing the fear in the man's eyes went a long way. Jake pressed his lips together, holding back everything he wanted to say as the wave of anger and frustration exploded inside.

Strong hands with thick fingers pried at Jake's biceps, at his hands around Burroughs's throat, the pain in his arm buried under his fury.

Now the guards wanted to pull him off. When they thought he might actually *kill* Burroughs. His grip loosened, allowing Burroughs to choke out his words.

"Get. Him. Off. Me."

The men shoved Jake against the wall. Would they hold him there and let Burroughs throw a few punches? His face crimson, Burroughs straightened his bow tie and cummerbund, and wiped the sweat from his forehead.

Gasping from his efforts, Jake's pulse hammered against his ribs as he tried to break free from the two men holding him, but they wouldn't budge.

"What's happening inside that room, Burroughs? You going to leave Kelsey in there alone? She trusted you. Who's calling the shots here, anyway?"

That's it. Fill the man's head with more doubt and confusion. Add to his dilemma. He would make a mistake soon enough.

"I'll take care of Kelsey. But you're a loose cannon. You cause more trouble than you're worth." Burroughs eyed the guard to Jake's right. "Take care of him."

Jake chuckled. "Take care of me? What does that mean? You're going to add my death to the list of your crimes? Do these men work for you or Ivanov?"

Without responding, Burroughs adjusted his jacket and placed his hand on the doorknob that would lead him back to Kelsey, even though he'd been kicked out, too.

The two guards tugged Jake away from Burroughs. Away from Kelsey and down the hall. They were both twice his size and he knew from experience if he struggled too much, he'd wake up hours later with a throbbing headache—if he woke up at all. He had to be smart. Use the chance that Kelsey had given him. But he kept his head angled to watch Burroughs for as long as he could.

The guy still hadn't entered the room. Jake was beginning to doubt he would.

Too soon they turned a corner and passed the party. Someone tried to exit, escorted by a guard, but the woman was quickly ushered back inside the room.

"Where are you taking me?" Jake asked.

"To get some fresh air."

That could be good. But it could also be bad. Initially, he'd wanted that—but on *his* terms. "Thought you were supposed to take me back to the party."

Cool air swept over him as they stepped above deck into the clear night sky, a reprieve from the overcast and drizzling weather that he and Kelsey had endured while making their way through the wilderness.

Jake started a mental rundown of possible outcomes to what Burroughs meant by, "take care of him."

He had a feeling it was all left up to interpretation. Sucking in a breath, he let out a sigh. "Now that's what I've needed all evening. Thanks for bringing me up."

The men released him, but he ducked his head at just the right moment, saving himself from a fist in the face. He'd developed a keen sense for what was coming.

Throwing his fist into one of the men's guts, he felt like he'd hit granite. The guy smiled. They both expected to have some fun with him, and then what, he wasn't sure. But he wasn't going to wait around to find out. He'd shake them first, and then find Kelsey and get her out of here.

"Sorry, I can't stick around for the fun." Jake took a flying leap off the yacht.

* * *

Kelsey didn't believe that this man knew nothing of her abduction. People didn't get where he was in life, obtain this much wealth and power, without knowing what was going on around them.

She wished he didn't. Wished he would call the police and this ordeal would be over. But she knew better.

"All this...for an old map?" Kelsey asked. "It is really worth people's lives?"

She wasn't sure when it had happened, but she'd lost her fear. She was tired of running. There was nothing left except for her to face the man ultimately responsible.

His shoulder shook with a soft chuckle, and a frank, knowing grin at the corners of his mouth. "You're a smart woman. But this has all been a misunderstanding. And it's not just an old map. It's a missing page from an antique book depicting the Ivanov heritage—a heritage that spans many centuries. This page, which holds the key to some aspects of the book, was stolen over a hundred years ago. And when I heard news of it and who held it, I contracted those I knew to have the best chance of success in retrieving it for me. Who would have access—a method and a path. But there was a problem."

Behind Ivanov, a door opened and Lennon stepped through it. Kelsey gasped. Ivanov smiled without glancing at Lennon—Jonathan Hunter.

Or was *that* even his name?

"This man claims he had the map, was bringing it to me, when you stole it from him."

A knock came at the door. "It's Davis," his muffled voice said through the door.

Ivanov ignored him.

Kelsey's head swam. "Stole from him? He's the one who tried to steal it. He's the one who kidnapped me, don't you see? I had nothing at all to do with the map. I didn't even know it existed. And what about Davis? Why don't you ask him? I don't know who stole from whom."

"I explained the delicate nature of this matter to Mr. Burroughs, but he neglected to handle things personally. His man Neely was intercepted trying to sell this important part of my family history to someone who hates me."

Imagine that.

"Then why didn't he just ask Davis what happened to the map? Why put me and my friend through all this? This man is lying to you."

Ivanov turned to Lennon and Lennon, wielding a weapon with a silencer, shot Ivanov in the chest. Kelsey's horror stifled her scream.

He sneered down at Kelsey. "You were right—I lied." Suddenly his accent had turned thick and Russian.

Confusion gripped her thoughts in a torrent—Lennon wasn't afraid to shoot Ivanov on his own boat, surrounded by his own guards? Was he crazy?

"You just shot Roman Ivanov." The walls tilted. "We're both going to die now."

"Wrong. You were going to die on this man's boat, but I came to get you out of here. Now you're going to show me what you did with the map." He was at her side, helping her up.

"I'm not going anywhere with you." Why hadn't he gone after Jake? Jake also knew where the map was. Unfortunately, Kelsey had an idea why Lennon came for her instead. Kelsey prayed Jake was still alive. Her trust in God, in Jake, now wavering again.

I will fear no evil.

Lennon thrust the muzzle of the gun under her chin and pressed hard. He peered at her, his face close, his eyes narrowing behind his glasses. He lifted an electroshock device. "I have ways to make you comply. Would you like to experience one of them?"

Kelsey couldn't breathe, but she could shake her head.

"Good, now come with me."

"Who are you? Really?"

"Viktor Orlov." He grinned, that familiar, hateful grin. "I work for Ivanov's brother—the man who hates him."

TWENTY-FOUR

Jake swam to the aft of the yacht, looking to gain access at the stern. The two guards hadn't jumped in after him, but they could still meet him at the stern, so he remained cautious. A boat powered up not fifteen yards from him—he'd recognize the sound of the eight hundred HP Volvo engine anywhere.

He tensed. Though it was too dark to see, he could hear well enough to just make out the severe displeasure in a woman's voice.

Kelsey!

Back on *The Buccaneer?*

The clouds drifted away from the moon and a man's face came into view. Jake would recognize those round glasses anywhere. Then Lennon disappeared behind the covered helm and the boat moved away, taking Kelsey with it. Jake had no clue how he'd gotten Kelsey from Ivanov.

The whine of a smaller boat starting up behind Jake drew his attention. Treading the cold water, he angled himself to catch sight of a speedboat near the stern of the yacht.

He swam toward the smaller craft with all the swiftness his tired, stiff limbs could muster, but he was fueled by adrenaline and the need to save Kelsey—the woman he loved. He dragged himself over the side and stealthily approached the bulk of a man at the wheel who then spun around to face him.

Kelsey's guard. The man's eyes grew wide when he spotted Jake.

"Hit me," the guy said.

Dripping wet, Jake shook off the cold fog in his head. "What?"

"You're going to save her right? You need to hit me, knock me overboard and take the boat from me."

Jake didn't think one punch would do it. "I don't have time to argue who's going to save her. Let's do it together."

"If I get to her first, I'll have to bring her back."

Why was the man doing this? *Dude, just quit your job.* But maybe one couldn't just quit from this operation. "Okay."

Jake swung his fist, full force, punching the guy in the nose. Kelsey's guard allowed himself to fall overboard. That had to be it.

Careful to avoid Kelsey's secret admirer, Jake steered the boat around and raced toward *The Buccaneer,* which headed to the dock and the city in the distance. He pushed it, full throttle.

Come on, come on, come on.

The racer could catch *The Buccaneer* easily enough, he'd experienced that already.

Everything that had happened before played back in his mind. This is where it all started, everything in reverse. Now he was doing the chasing. Good thing Kelsey's admirer had left his gun resting in the seat. As his target drew closer, he chambered a round, but Lennon fired on him first. Jake wasn't about to shoot and put Kelsey in danger. He would just have to make his way onto the other boat.

This time, he had to save the day, and if he gave Kelsey the chance to flee to safety, he needed her to take it. He hoped she'd be willing to let him save her, to leave him behind.

Gripping the wheel, he rammed the racer into the bigger boat and immediately launched on to the flattened stern. Lennon met him head-on. Jake wasn't too worried. This was the guy who didn't fight himself, but enjoyed watching.

You should have kept Flanagan, then this would be a real battle.

Jake allowed the rage that had boiled inside since the beginning of this ordeal to erupt and flung himself at Lennon.

Both men lost their weapons in the clash. Lennon escaped Jake's grip and jumped up the steps to the helm, with Jake on his heels. When Jake slammed into him again, *The Buccaneer* lurched forward. He pushed the wheel counterclockwise and the small cruiser yacht turned in a wide arc away from the dock and people, and toward the dark horizon. Lennon had to have put it on autopilot, needing to make good on his escape from Ivanov's boat.

Jake pounded Lennon's face, crushing his glasses while the yacht sped forward into the dark water ahead.

But then strong arms lifted him and threw him, his back hitting a hard edge. Racking pain paralyzed him for precious seconds. He couldn't react, or respond to Flanagan who grinned and reached for him.

Jake was better than this. Head, guts, *heart.* But he needed more than his own willpower, his own inner strength. He had to draw on something much more than that, or Someone.

When I am weak, You are strong! God help me, by Your saving grace.

Jake fingered the steak knife in his pocket and pulled it out, angling it at Flanagan.

"You're going to kill me with a steak knife?" the big guy asked through his laugh.

Then Flanagan froze, his muscles spasming as he fell to the ground. Kelsey stood at the entrance below deck, holding the electroshock device, the projectiles still extending from her to Flanagan. Jake nodded, relieved she was okay, but this wasn't over. He scraped his body from the deck, aware of Lennon searching for his weapon, his cracked glasses hanging crooked from his face. He grabbed the gun as Jake rushed him, pinning him against the dash panel. If only he could shock Lennon and incapacitate him, too, until the authorities came.

Lennon slammed his fist into Jake's arm.

Blinding pain flashed in his mind. He sank to the floor, his body refusing to obey his commands. Lennon shoved his broken glasses in place and grinned—that horrible grin.

He gripped his weapon. Jake knew what was coming next. There was only one thing he could do—

He inched his hand up, stretching, his muscles screaming until he reached the throttle and shoved it forward. Lennon lost his balance with the sudden lurch. When Jake kicked him in the gut, Lennon fell against the wheel, giving Jake a chance to grab his gun.

Kelsey stood over Flanagan, keeping him at her mercy, but when she glanced toward the helm, her eyes widened. "The rocks are dead ahead!"

"Jump! Release Flanagan and jump." It was the only way.

But she just stood there, frozen.

Ignoring the pain, Jake forced himself up. Before Lennon could react, Jake raced toward Kelsey and made to jump, but something snagged his leg.

He looked down.

Flanagan.

The man's eyes pleaded. Ritter's face flashed in Jake's mind. He looked back at Lennon. He couldn't save them all, but Lennon only glared at him from the wheel. The man had control—he could veer them away from the rocky shore ahead, if he would only realize what was dead ahead of him.

Mercy trumps judgment.

Jake hefted Flanagan up and looked at Kelsey.

Together they hurled themselves into the air as *The Buccaneer* raced into rocky outcropping ahead.

* * *

Fiery flames filled the night as Kelsey swam toward the surface. She breached the water and gasped for breath, thankful they'd made the jump mere seconds before impact.

"Are you okay?" Jake's voice called from behind.

Treading water, Kelsey swung around. "Yes."

He held on to Flanagan. "I have to swim to shore, help Flanagan."

She nodded, saving her breath and energy. They had a swim ahead of them, but fortunately, they could make the shore without having to worry about the waves and current forcing them against the rocks here.

Above them, a helicopter whirred and lights searched the waters. Jake made shore before Kelsey, signaled to the chopper above and then swam back out to her. When they were able to touch bottom, he lifted her in his arms and carried her forward.

She wrapped her arms around his neck and pressed her face into his good shoulder. Then she remembered. "Where's Flanagan?"

Flashlights glared in her eyes and men flocked around them, shouting.

"Looks like he's caught in a net of lawmen," Jake said. "My oldest brother found us. I see Reg and…is that…*Eric?*"

"You can put me down now," she said.

"No, I can't." He smiled at her, sending a shiver over her that had nothing to do with the cold water.

"Okay, break it up now." Reg stood next to them along with Eric.

Too soon Jake set her down, but his arms held her tight against him. "Just conducting some personal business," he said and winked at her.

"What are you doing here, Eric?" Kelsey asked. She'd hoped to keep him out of this, but she'd obviously failed.

"He's the reason we're here," Reg offered. "He called the police."

Eric stepped forward now. "It's my fault you ended up back in the hands of those men. I should have told you from the beginning, but I had planned to stall you, keep you from leaving until I could figure out how to keep you safe. I should have warned you."

I have to keep them from leaving... Kelsey remembered his words. But he'd said them meaning to protect them? She groaned inside. They'd had it all wrong. "I don't understand."

"My nephew is the deputy at Hood. I knew he was involved in a smuggling operation with Davis Burroughs. Then my aunt found me and told me what he'd done with you."

"And you turned him in?" Kelsey was aghast. Eric gave up his hiding place and his nephew?

"I couldn't sit by and do nothing. Figured I've been missing in action for too long." He looked at Jake, a twinkle in his eye. "You talk in your sleep."

"Speaking of which, I think I've been out of action too long, too." Jake whisked her back into his arms.

What was with him carrying her? But she loved it.

"I love you, Kelsey Chambers."

"And I love you. I trust you with my life and…my heart." How could she not after everything this man had been through for her and with her?

Ignoring all the commotion around them, he pressed his forehead against hers. "You're the only woman I've ever loved, and will ever love. I want you, I *need* you, to be my wife. What do you say? Willing to give us a second chance?"

"Chances like this only come once in a lifetime. I hope you can trust me to stand by that, this time."

He grinned and pressed his lips against hers, kissing her like a man who'd found a long-lost treasure.

And Kelsey had found hers.

My cup overflows. Surely goodness and loving-kindness will follow me all the days of my life...

* * * * *

Dear Reader

I love to travel and have always thought that being a travel writer would be a dream job. But I also love adventure so I thought it would be great fun to throw a little adventure at my heroine, Kelsey Chambers. In *Riptide,* she faces more obstacles than she could ever have imagined, and she's far from prepared to handle any of them. But in the midst of her troubles, God is there, holding her hand all the way through, and she especially understands that when she sees the verses from Psalm 23 staring at her from Eric's Bible.

God sends us what we need to help us through at just the right time. Not too early and not too late. I know this from my own life experience and I write this into my stories with confidence.

As for Jake, he has found a way to tackle his issues, believing himself strong, but in the end his methods will only carry him so far. He finally understands that there is only One who can see him through, just as the Lord tells us in Isaiah 43:2: *When you pass through the waters, I will be with you; and when you pass through the rivers, they will not sweep over you. When you walk through the fire, you will not be burned; the flames will not set you ablaze.*

I hope you enjoyed *Riptide,* and I pray many blessings over your life.

Elizabeth Goddard

www.elizabethgoddard.com

Questions for Discussion

1. In *Riptide,* Kelsey is working as a travel writer—a job she hoped would get her mind and heart off a failed relationship. Has there been a time in your life when you had to take extra measures in order to move on? Explain.

2. The job Kelsey takes ends up putting her right back in Jake's path—the very man she had hoped to forget. Have you ever been in a situation where you ran into someone you wanted to avoid, and then perhaps were forced to work out your differences? Discuss what happened.

3. Jake is a man who has lost his way when it comes to his relationship with God. That loss of his sense of direction has worked to affect everything in his life. Has there been a time in your life when you felt like you had lost your way? What happened?

4. Kelsey has trust issues because of her experience with her father. Are there people in your life whom you struggle to trust? How did you work through it?

5. Because of the way Kelsey's father had treated her mother, she fears trusting Jake, a man who is popular with the women. Do you understand her struggle? Why or why not?

6. Kelsey and Jake are caught in a situation they could never have imagined or prepared for, and even when they escape into the Olympic Wilderness, they are hardly prepared to face the elements. Do you think they made the right decision when they escaped the boat? How would you have handled things differently?

7. What would you do if you found yourself lost in a wilderness area with nothing more than a first aid kit?

8. Think back to Kelsey's decision to save Jake instead of closing the distance to the sheriff's office. Those would have been the longest steps of her life. Would you have handled it differently? How and why?

9. What was your initial impression of Eric? Would you have trusted him? Why or why not?

10. Discuss your thoughts on Kelsey and Jake's relationship problems and the dynamics that broke them up and kept them apart.

11. How important do you think trust is in a relationship? At what point does a person deserve to be trusted? Why or why not?

12. Kelsey's both stunned and disappointed when she learns how her boss and friend, Davis Burroughs, has treated her, by putting her in the middle of his smuggling operation. Have you ever had anyone put you into an awkward position? What happened?

13. Jake relies heavily on himself to make it through this crisis until he finally realizes that he needs to rely on God to help him through. Has there ever been a time in your life where you thought you were strong enough to take care of things on your own until you realized that only God could help you? What did you learn from that experience? Discuss.

14. Through the story, Jake has to rise up to his "noble cause" to struggle against an impossible situation in

order to save the woman he loves—a woman he hasn't even decided he's willing to open his heart up to again. What is your impression of him? Do you see him as a hero? Why or why not?

15. Do you think the experience that Kelsey went through with Jake is enough to mend their broken relationship, or rather, enough for her to finally trust him?

REQUEST YOUR FREE BOOKS!
2 FREE RIVETING INSPIRATIONAL NOVELS
PLUS 2 FREE MYSTERY GIFTS

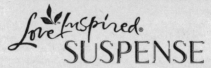

YES! Please send me 2 FREE Love Inspired® Suspense novels and my 2 FREE mystery gifts (gifts are worth about $10). After receiving them, if I don't wish to receive any more books, I can return the shipping statement marked "cancel." If I don't cancel, I will receive 4 brand-new novels every month and be billed just $4.74 per book in the U.S. or $5.24 per book in Canada. That's a savings of at least 21% off the cover price. It's quite a bargain! Shipping and handling is just 50¢ per book in the U.S. and 75¢ per book in Canada.* I understand that accepting the 2 free books and gifts places me under no obligation to buy anything. I can always return a shipment and cancel at any time. Even if I never buy another book, the two free books and gifts are mine to keep forever.

123/323 IDN F5AC

Name	(PLEASE PRINT)	

Address		Apt. #

City	State/Prov.	Zip/Postal Code

Signature (if under 18, a parent or guardian must sign)

Mail to the **Harlequin® Reader Service:**
IN U.S.A.: P.O. Box 1867, Buffalo, NY 14240-1867
IN CANADA: P.O. Box 609, Fort Erie, Ontario L2A 5X3

**Are you a current subscriber to Love Inspired Suspense books
and want to receive the larger-print edition?
Call 1-800-873-8635 or visit www.ReaderService.com.**

* Terms and prices subject to change without notice. Prices do not include applicable taxes. Sales tax applicable in N.Y. Canadian residents will be charged applicable taxes. Offer not valid in Quebec. This offer is limited to one order per household. Not valid for current subscribers to Love Inspired Suspense books. All orders subject to credit approval. Credit or debit balances in a customer's account(s) may be offset by any other outstanding balance owed by or to the customer. Please allow 4 to 6 weeks for delivery. Offer available while quantities last.

Your Privacy—The Harlequin® Reader Service is committed to protecting your privacy. Our Privacy Policy is available online at www.ReaderService.com or upon request from the Harlequin Reader Service.
We make a portion of our mailing list available to reputable third parties that offer products we believe may interest you. If you prefer that we not exchange your name with third parties, or if you wish to clarify or modify your communication preferences, please visit us at www.ReaderService.com/consumerchoice or write to us at Harlequin Reader Service Preference Service, P.O. Box 9062, Buffalo, NY 14269. Include your complete name and address.

LIS13R

SPECIAL EXCERPT FROM

Love Inspired

*Brian Montclair is about to go from
factory worker to baker.*

Read on for a sneak preview of
THE BACHELOR BAKER
by Carolyne Aarsen, the second book in
THE HEART OF MAIN STREET *series from*
Love Inspired. Available August 2013!

He took up her whole office.

At least that's how it felt to Melissa Sweeney.

Brian Montclair sat in the chair across from her, his arms folded over his chest, his entire demeanor screaming "get me out of here."

Tall with broad shoulders and arms filling out his button-down shirt rolled up at the sleeves, he looked more like a linebacker than a potential baker's assistant.

Which is what he might become if he took the job Melissa had to offer him.

Melissa held up the worn and dog-eared paper she had been given. It held a short list of potential candidates for the job at her bakery.

The rest of the names had been crossed off with comments written beside them. Unsuitable. Too old. Unable to be on their feet all day. Just had a baby. Nut allergy. Moved away.

This last comment appeared beside two of the eight names on her list, a sad commentary on the state of the town of Bygones.

When Melissa had received word of a mysterious

LIEXP0713

benefactor offering potential business owners incentive money to start up a business in the small town of Bygones, Kansas, she had immediately applied. All her life she had dreamed of starting up her own bakery. She had taken courses in baking, decorating, business management, all with an eye to someday living out the faint dream of owning her own business.

When she had been approved, she'd quit her job in St. Louis, packed up her few belongings and had come here. She felt as if her life had finally taken a good turn. However, in the past couple of weeks it had become apparent that she needed extra help.

She had received the list of potential hires from the Bygones Save Our Street Committee and was told to try each of them. Brian Montclair was on the list. At the bottom, but still on the list.

"The reason I called you here was to offer you a job," she said, trying to inject a note of enthusiasm into her voice. This had better work.

To find out if Melissa and Brian can help save the town of Bygones one cupcake at a time, pick up
THE BACHELOR BAKER
wherever Love Inspired books are sold.

Love Inspired.
SUSPENSE
RIVETING INSPIRATIONAL ROMANCE

Years after her daughter's abduction, skip tracer Erica James has a new suspect—Max Powell's missing sister. Together Erica and Max search for answers, but the kidnapper will do anything to keep them from finding Erica's daughter—including murder.

HIDE AND SEEK
by
LYNETTE EASON

Available August 2013 wherever
Love Inspired Suspense books are sold.

www.LoveInspiredBooks.com

LIS44548

Both Abbey Harris and Dominic Winters long for a second chance at love, and it'll take two adorable dogs and a sweet little girl to bring them together.

Healing Hearts
by Margaret Daley

Available August 2013
wherever Love Inspired books are sold.

LI87830